Legogote

A story with its roots in the Lowveld of South Africa

By Peter Lewis

This story is dedicated to my late father-in-law Ismail Rajah 1928-2016, who might have been the Indian man in Chapter 10. Ismail loved the Lowveld and its people.

Foreword

Legogote is set in present day South Africa while making frequent visits to the Apartheid era when formative experiences of the key protagonists laid the ground for the events described here.

South Africa today is a disappointed country. The optimism of the immediate period after the first democratic election in 1994 has long since evaporated. Nelson Mandela has left us. Corruption has pervaded everyday life and left ordinary people deeply cynical. The press in South Africa has a proud history. Investigative journalism, dramatized in what follows, is making a vital contribution to the exposure of wrong doing, defence of free speech and leading a vibrant national discourse.

The South Africa of the seventies was in a time warp, set in aspic, where colonial attitudes to race had been solidified into a legal system which was a disaster for the entire population even if the privileged white citizens did not fully appreciate it at the time. The system survived longer than it should have as the regime was able to represent itself as a bastion against communism in southern Africa and western powers tempered their disapproval accordingly.

Some of the passages describing the life and death of the elder Doctor were originally published in an eponymous short story. He really did work as a glassware washer in a Government laboratory but that is where the similarities between this story and his real life probably end. The truth is, I do not know what happened to the real senior Doctor. Hopefully, he did not suffer the same violent end. Almost certainly, he did face years of struggle and risks to his longevity from the Apartheid state, township violence,

2

AIDS or the poverty that is still endemic after more than a quarter of a century of freedom.

I pray that the real Doctor, our hero's father, had a long and fulfilling life and that he and his progeny are today enjoying the fruits of freedom for which so many South Africans made sacrifices; freedom which is still tenuous and under threat from different but nevertheless malevolent forces to those at work four decades ago.

Chapter 1
Return to the Lowveld

Doctor is relieved to be leaving Johannesburg. The short, but intense, Highveld winter is getting him down. His tiny Brixton bedsit is alternately freezing cold and oppressively hot and fume-filled from the paraffin heater that he uses in the evenings. The days are dazzlingly sunny and quite warm but not enough to lift his African spirits. His work as a freelance journalist is going well though the nature of the stories he writes add to his depression. He spends his days probing into the morass of corruption that is threatening to suck the lifeblood out of his country. It is one such story that is giving him the excuse to leave the city and head for his recently rediscovered homeland in The Lowveld.

Doctor picks up a small holdall and heads downstairs to the scruffy street where he opens the boot of a white Polo sedan. His writing has earned him enough to afford this old but reliable car and he is happy that, for the moment at least, he does not have to rely on public transport or hitched rides. Moving round to the driver's door, he notices a ragged young man approaching and he slides his long frame into the seat and slams the door in the hope of moving off before any trouble can threaten his, so far, quiet day. Potential trouble is already tapping on the window and putting his hand to his mouth as if taking a few fingers of mealie pap. Doctor checks the small change in the ash tray, normally reserved for parking guards, winds down half the window and pragmatically hands over a two-rand coin. He is God Blessed and keeps his quiet start to the day in exchange. It is not so long ago that he too was begging for food and small change to stay alive.

The Polo is soon on its way out of the city heading east on the N12; passing under several e-toll gantries between Gillooly's and Putfontein; Starling to Ugaga. Each gantry is named for a bird. The tolls amount to a few rand but they will not be collected. For almost everyone in the city, including Doctor, they are the object of petty civil disobedience and a demonstration of people power. The grievances and resentments of metro South Africans are distilled into this small, every day, defiance. The task of enforcing the tolls is as impossible as was preventing ordinary, unarmed, Germans from demolishing the Berlin Wall, three decades ago.

Doctor is happy to be warm and lulled by the telephone talk show on SA FM. Lulled, that is, until he hears a familiar voice shouting his indignation about the latest misspending of public funds. The voice is one of his better contacts and responsible for pointing him in the direction of his current investigation.

Released from the city congestion and out into the straw-coloured East Rand, past Springs, the aging Polo is easily through the speed limit. Doctor is thankful again to the elderly, previous owner who religiously serviced the car for fifteen years while covering just eighty thousand klicks. The arrow straight road only undulates as it processes across the Highveld and then, after Machadodorp, starts its rapid, ear popping, descent towards the Lowveld. Spring is still a month away so there is no chance of any rain.

Four hours later, Doctor guides his prized car into the yard of his aunt's little house in KaBokweni. No one is at home so he wanders down the hill to a café and buys a couple of oranges and a Kit-Kat which will be his lunch. He carefully averts his eyes while passing the bottle store and hurries back up the hill. His spirits are already on the rise thanks to the extra five degrees of warmth that the lower altitude is allowing.

On his return, he finds his cousin's wife, Bongile, in the yard, about to let herself into the house. She has a new born baby slung on her back and encircled by a blanket in the traditional way. They greet cheerfully. It is only the second time they have met but she is expecting him.

Bongile boils some water for tea on the two-ring stove and settles to feed the baby, a girl, in the shade of a tree in the yard. Doctor shares his Kit-Kat with her and they talk casually about the state of affairs locally and the whereabouts of the rest of the household. Doctor observes that the mains water has been restored since his last visit. Bongile recalls the strikes and tyre burning protests back in May that, combined with refilled dams, had persuaded the municipality to restore the supply.

Shortly, another cousin's wife arrives, also with a baby on her back. Doctor notices that Precious already appears to be pregnant again.

By the time the sun has set, the family is reunited for the evening. Doctor is happy to find his Aunt Funi is in good health and while she prepares supper, they talk about the months that have passed since his first visit.

The evening is chilly but not cold. The Lukhele household improvise chairs and gather around the small fold up dining cum picnic table to welcome Doctor and eat the frugal fare that Funi has prepared. At the end of the meal, Funi proudly brings a large, jam filled, homemade sponge cake to the table and announces that it is to celebrate Doctor's return. Combined with hot, sweet tea, the cake makes a satisfying end to the meal.

The sleeping arrangements have got more difficult since the arrival of the two new babies and Doctor is offered the battered sofa and a blanket. Curling himself to fit between the arms of the sofa, he is soon asleep and does not hear the babies cry when they wake for their feeds in the early hours.

Chapter 2
Joy

The next morning, after most of the household has already left for work, Doctor drives fifteen downhill kilometres to Mbombela, the sprawling provincial capital that sits in a bowl surrounded by hills. At the robots controlling the major intersection in town, he is surprised to see a skinny, sunburnt Afrikaner man begging between the lines of stationary vehicles. At the next lights, he sees a white woman also begging. He guesses they are husband and wife. In the past, the man would have had a protected job for life, perhaps on the railways; now he is probably unemployable.

Doctor sets himself up in a coffee shop in town and connects his laptop to the free wi-fi. Then he dials the number that his contact from the previous day's talk show had given him. A woman answers. He confirms that she is Joy and explains that he is hoping to talk to her; maybe over a coffee or lunch. Joy is at work and her hushed tone makes it apparent that she is reluctant to say much over the phone. Joy agrees to meet him just after noon.

Doctor slowly consumes his coffee, making it last for nearly two hours, while finishing a piece he has been writing about the misappropriation of school funds. He hopes to sell the piece to The Sunday Times.

Joy Mpofu arrives at the agreed time. She is a stout, middle-aged woman who greets him cautiously but not without some warmth. She mentions that she has read some of his stories in the papers.

Joy works for the Provincial Government as a clerk in the HR department. She has been in her job for ten years and as her husband is a self-employed electrician, they have a combined income that allows them to take out a bond on a small house in a gated complex in Dlamini, just out of town. They can even afford a nearly new Toyota as well as the bakkie that her husband uses for his business. Doctor shuffles self-consciously and tries to hide his battered tekkies that suggest he is significantly less affluent.

Joy chooses a toasted cheese sarmie on brown with ice tea and Doctor orders the same. Although the coffee shop is filling up with lunchtime customers from local offices, they are sat at a table which offers a degree of privacy. She describes her role in HR where she is responsible for checking that employee expenses have been completed with the necessary receipts and approval signatures. She then sets up the payment to the employee's bank account and files the claim. She is also responsible for sending claims over two years old to the archives for another eight years in case of future audit checks.

Earlier in the winter, Doctor had met his talk show contact, Abu, at the Zoo Lake in the affluent suburbs of Johannesburg. They had walked in brilliant sunshine while talking about the constitutional crisis which was constantly simmering but never quite coming to a head. Abu has been an active ANC member all his adult life. Now he is angry with the younger generation of leaders who seem to have forgotten their history. At a point in their walk, when they were totally alone, they stopped. His companion changed the subject, mentioning that he had recently been involved in some work with the Mpumalanga Provincial Government. When checking out at the end of his last visit, the bill for his modest guest house stay had already been settled by the client. The paid bill had been proffered and then quickly withdrawn, but not before he noticed it was larger than he would have expected. At most, the bill for three nights' bed and breakfast should have been fifteen hundred rand. The actual bill was nearly ten thousand.

Abu had queried the hotel bill with the government official he was working with. She promised to follow up but seemed neither surprised nor concerned.

A few weeks later, Abu had received a call from Joy Mpofu. After a few pleasantries, Joy explained that she was processing the expense claim related to his guesthouse bill which had been submitted by the same government official who had hosted him during the recent work. She asked Abu if there was any reason he could think of for the large bill that his stay had incurred. He could not and he mentioned that he too had queried the bill before leaving the Government offices. Without knowing why, Joy left her office phone number with Abu and rang off hurriedly; apparently reluctant to get involved in further discussion.

Joy has launched into her side of the same story when the sarmies arrive. When they are alone again, she resumes. Abu's government official had relocated from a similar role in Gauteng about a year ago. Her monthly expenses were always noticeably higher than most of her colleagues. At first, Joy rationalised this was due to the cost of relocation and her temporary accommodation. After 6 months, the trend continued and the amounts got larger still; significantly higher, in fact, than her salary. The expenses were always approved by the same boss and Joy noticed that when he was on vacation, the expense reports were delayed pending his return rather than approved by his stand-in which would have been normal.

Finishing her iced tea, Joy reaches into her handbag and passes a folded copy of the guesthouse expense claim to Doctor. Abu's Government official is April Coetzee and her boss is Lucas Nozulu.

Joy makes her excuses, thanks Doctor for lunch and hurries away.

Chapter 3
The Guest House

Doctor pays the bill for the long-forgotten coffee and the light lunch and heads back to his car. The parking guard impatiently guides him out of the space and gratefully receives the customary small change in return.

The guesthouse is about five hundred metres up a sand road off the main road to the airport near Plaston. The extensive gardens are neat and will be lush again soon when the spring rains arrive. Doctor is greeted enthusiastically by a Jack Russell terrier and then coolly by a white woman who introduces herself as the owner. Doctor explains that he is searching for a job as a receptionist. She looks at him sceptically, perhaps because his scruffy appearance does not immediately suggest he would be appealing to her newly arrived guests. His clipped speaking voice, refined during his varsity studies, is at odds with her first impression but she does not need a receptionist. Her business, with just five comfortably luxurious rooms, is too small.

Doctor feigns disappointment, thanks the owner and turns to leave.

Walking slowly back to his car, a recent black Audi bumps gingerly up the sand road towards him. The car's plates immediately attract his attention; Nozulu MP.

A tall, suited man eases himself out of the car and heads for the reception. Doctor leans against his car and pretends to make a call. A few minutes later, the presumed Lucas Nozulu makes his way to a chalet in the grounds, unlocks its front door and disappears from view. Apparently, he has no luggage.

As Doctor returns to the Plaston Road, he is forced to move off the track to give way to a white Range Rover. The driver's window is down giving him a clear view of a blonde woman, in her mid-thirties, wearing expensive sunglasses. She pays him no attention as she sweeps past. Doctor reflects that she is surely more used to five-star hotels than this more modest resting place.

Returning to KaBokweni, Doctor forgets, for the moment, his afternoon encounters and enjoys the warmth of his family for a second night. Bongile, cousin Promise's wife, has apparently acquired some new skills since his late summer visit and presents a hearty chicken stew with mealie pap. Aunt Funi's small home is infused with the smell of the slow cooked food and there is a sense of security which, although temporary, is very comforting. For the moment, no amount of money or luxury trappings could beat the cosy glow that Doctor is experiencing.

The next morning is very warm suggesting that winter is nearly over and that Spring may be passed over altogether. The sky is completely cloudless, however, so the rains will not be bringing their greening miracle for a while yet.

Doctor drives back towards Plaston; parking the Polo under a fever tree on the verge, close to the sand road leading to the Guest House. He goes over the plan in his mind and frets that he may be about to break the law in order to further his investigation but he has convinced himself, already several times, that the ends justify the means.

Leaving his car, he walks through the long, dry grass and the Macadamia trees planted in the land adjoining the house and makes his way round to the back without being noticed by anyone or the resident Jack Russell. A guineafowl makes its haunting, southern African call as it rushes from under his feet. He notices the parking area is empty. Settling down out of sight, against a rock about twenty-five metres from the kitchen, from which emanates some gentle hymn singing, he basks in the warm sunshine. An unseen Laughing Dove repeats its signature, reassuring chuckle.

After a few minutes, the owner of the hymn singing voice emerges from the kitchen and throws some potato peelings onto a compost heap in the kitchen garden. As she does so, a gardener appears from an outbuilding and starts a conversation with his colleague. It appears to be a seductive discussion. The young woman is giggling in response to the gardener's banter.

The flirtation comes to an end and the two staff members go back to their work.

Doctor leaves his hiding place and makes his way round to the front, entering the reception. The absence of any cars encourages him to believe that the owner is away and that all the guests have already checked out. He can hear the hymn singing voice again; apparently still accompanying the food preparation for the evening to come. Doctor slips into the small back office behind the reception desk. He scans the office. A number of box files stand tidily in a wall mounted book case. One is labelled "Guest Bills 2017" and another "Suppliers Invoices 2017".

Doctor opens the first box and shuffles through the bills. They are mostly for one-night stays and typically in the range eight hundred to a thousand rand. Several though, are for much larger amounts. Abu's bill is one of them.

A newly acquired smart phone records the exceptional bills. Then he turns to the supplier invoices, most of which are for food supplies. He notices that once a month there is an invoice for "marketing services" and the amounts are typically around thirty thousand rand. The invoice is in the name of a company called Promovest with a registered office in Johannesburg.

As he is about to photograph a couple of the Promovest invoices, Doctor hears a car approaching up the sand road. Replacing the box files, Doctor heads for the voice in the kitchen. He slips out of the kitchen door, into the garden, but not without breaking the reverie of the young woman who looks up from her food preparation and screams. She reaches the kitchen door just after Doctor makes it back to his hiding place.

The gardener has obviously heard the scream because he joins the woman by the kitchen door and then shortly afterwards the owner emerges from the side of the house. It must have been the sound of her car that curtailed Doctor's espionage. The Jack Russell is also back.

There is a short discussion between the owner and her staff. The gardener then moves tentatively towards the Macadamia trees perhaps in the hope of finding some evidence of the intruder. The owner makes a short phone call. Fortunately, the Jack Russell seems oblivious to the excitement and sits grooming himself rather than lending his superior senses to the task in hand.

Doctor stays hidden. The gardener's half-hearted search comes within a few metres of his position without revealing it. After a few minutes, he gives up with a shrug of the shoulders. Doctor starts to move back towards his car, taking advantage of the cover provided by the long dry grass from the previous summer.

Before he can reach the Polo, Doctor is forced to drop down onto the ground. A couple of private security guards are getting out of their bakkie and looking around the car. Doctor guesses they are responding to the call from the guesthouse owner. The guards are armed with hand guns and they start to make a beeline for the house across the veld. This takes them close to his position but not close enough and Doctor is able to watch them as they make a theatrically paramilitary sweep of the area. He cannot help thinking that the gardener better not make any sudden moves or he will likely get shot.

The owner greets the gun toting men in the kitchen garden and a short discussion ensues. All three disappear into the house. Surely it would have made sense for one of the guards to continue scanning the veld for movement.

Doctor makes a run for his car about two hundred metres away. The gardener spots him and shouts an alarm. As he starts the car, throws it into first gear and moves away, Doctor sees the guards reappear and run in the direction of their bakkie. They will have his Gauteng registration number but it was another mistake to leave their vehicle so far from the house. Doctor is out of sight long before they are able to attempt a pursuit. Doctor is happy that he has been delinquent in registering the Polo's recent change of ownership. That will at least slow down any attempt to trace him that way. Anyway, when the owner confirms that nothing has been stolen, the investigation will end. The guards will probably deal with half a dozen similar calls today.

Chapter 4
Armed Response

The drive to the Provincial Administration buildings, just outside and north of Mbombela, takes only a few minutes. The buildings are next to the striking Legislature building which resembles the traditional beehive shaped huts of Swazi tribesmen who once hunted in this area.

The Polo does not look out of place in the visitors' car park where there is a normal cross section of cars ranging from battered, late twentieth century, good runners to newer but mostly modest models. In contrast, the adjacent staff car park is devoid of anything over ten years old and includes a liberal sprinkling of top of the range Mercedes, Range Rovers, BMWs and Audis. Doctor scans the staff car park and quickly spots Lucas Nozulu's black Audi. He has almost completed his survey before he locates the Range Rover of the woman that drove past him on the sand road the previous afternoon.

Before he leaves, Doctor calls Abu and gives him an update on his findings so far.

Doctor is happy with his day's work. He takes the road north out of Mbombela towards KaBokweni. Outside White River, he spots the Armed Response bakkie parked on the verge. Its two, not very professional, occupants are leant against the cab; each smoking. They are professional enough to recognise his car. In a second, the bakkie is on the road and closing in on the Polo.

Doctor pulls in realising that he cannot outrun the guards. The bakkie pulls round in front of the Polo and at an angle, making a rapid escape impossible. The two guards pull their guns and motion to Doctor to get out of the car. He complies and tries a cheerful Sawubona.

"Yebo." The two guards respond in unison. The driver asks him what he was doing on the Plaston Road this morning. Doctor mentions that he is looking for a job. What was he doing in the Guest House and why did he run? Doctor shrugs. He had been alone in reception. The return of the owner had made him panic; she would most likely suspect him of some petty theft simply because he was there alone. The guards can identify with that. "Why are you driving a car with Gauteng plates?" Doctor explains that he is staying with his aunt's family in KaBokweni while he tries to find a job.

"Who is your aunt?"

"She is Funi Lukhele. I am Doctor Lukhele." The guards relax. They know the Lukhele brothers; Doctor's cousins.

"OK then; go well. Maybe we will see you in the shebeen."

And maybe you won't, the recovering Doctor thinks to himself.

On the approach to his aunt's home, Doctor's phone rings. It is his editor at the Sunday Times. They are going to publish his just finished article this Sunday. He had better be ready for some social media reaction from the people that the article fingers. Or worse. His fee will be in his account early next week.

Doctor decides to call into the cash and carry and get some groceries for his family.

The evening is spent dealing with a new crisis. Cousin Promise's job in Mbombela laying fibre optic cable is coming to an end after six months. Without the money he has been earning, the family will struggle. He may have to join his brother and the dozens of men from KaBokweni that stand on street corners in White River and Mbombela in the hope of getting work, one day at a time, from a passing householder or small contractor in need of an extra pair of hands. The family has lots of ideas but nothing concrete that Promise can follow up. They all agree to ask around and see what opportunities might be coming up.

Trying to sleep on the undersized sofa later that night, Doctor thinks back to the time not so long ago when he was trying to stay sober and find work to help him get his mind straight and keep body and soul together. His descent into alcoholism had been a long one. He could not really pin-point when heavy drinking became a destructive addiction. He had broken up from his long-time girlfriend a few years ago but he could no longer be sure whether drink was part of the problem or was it the break up that had fuelled his habit. He had got into debt and been evicted from the apartment he rented. He joined the small army of homeless people in Jo'burg's Downtown. Eventually, an old varsity friend had taken pity on him and let him stay in the servants' cottage in his home in Sandton. He started a relentless fitness regime; running ten kilometres every morning and making full use of weights that his friend had bought with good intentions but abandoned some time ago. He succeeded in drying out without joining one of those soul baring groups that he had heard about. He knew that he had to steer clear of drink for the rest of his life and, in the last twelve months, things had gone well for him so that he was not often tempted to backslide. His restless mind continues to rehearse the events of the last year until he drifts into a deep sleep.

Abu calls early the next morning. He has checked out Promovest at CIPRO in Pretoria and discovered that the business is owned by Morne and April Coetzee.

Doctor calls the number he has for the guest house. He recognizes the voice of the owner who picks up. Doctor explains that they had met briefly two days ago and that, in fact, he is a freelance journalist rather than the unlikely hotel receptionist. The owner is annoyed by his deception. She threatens to end the conversation but Doctor manages to hold her attention by asking about her relationship with April Coetzee.

The guesthouse owner is Mrs. Raworth. April Coetzee is a regular client and nothing else. Doctor points out that she is a regular client whose company is in receipt of monthly payments from the guest house bank account. Mrs. Raworth ends the call. She has nothing more to say and Doctor should mind his own business.

Minutes later, his phone rings. The caller number is unknown. It is April Coetzee. She sounds calm and quite charming as she introduces herself and mentions his conversation with Mrs. Raworth. How can she help?

Doctor explains that he is curious about the relationship between Promovest and the guest house and its use as preferred lodging for consultants working with the Provincial Administration. April, still calm but less charming now, dismisses his curiosity by describing this as a perfectly normal business relationship. Doctor points out that since she is a co- owner of Promovest there may be a conflict of interest. Her interest has been declared to her boss so there is no issue. Doctor enquires whether that would be the same boss that she met at the guesthouse in the late afternoon of the day before yesterday. There is a silence. Then April angrily suggests that Doctor should be careful and that if she hears from him again she will be calling her attorney. The line goes dead.

Chapter 5
Lefa

Doctor turns his mind to the weekend. He must meet the evening Lowveld Link minibus arriving in White River from Joburg. He is in White River with plenty of time to spare and he has time to think over the last few days and his findings. Has he uncovered the whole story or opened the top of a can of worms? He cannot tell yet but he sketches a plan in his mind for the next steps in his investigation. The next week is going to be interesting and maybe dangerous.

His thoughts are interrupted by the arrival of the minibus. Seven or eight weary passengers disembark and collect their luggage from the trailer. One of the passengers is a Zulu woman in her late 50s. She is slim, quite tall, with beaded hair braids. She is smartly dressed and has obviously just applied fresh lipstick. She wears no jewellery. It is Doctor's mother, Lefa. They hug each other enthusiastically. Doctor takes her bag and they walk arm in arm to the white Polo.

During the twenty-minute drive to KaBokweni, Lefa describes her journey from Johannesburg and waxes lyrical about the mountains and the escarpment that transfixed her as she approached the Lowveld. Lefa has never travelled far from Joburg. A church trip to Potchefstroom is the limit of her travels. She knows only the Highveld, predominantly flat with its rocky kopjes, and heaved, at the beginning of time, nearly two kilometres above the seabed. The scenery of today's journey is on a different scale and she loves it. Doctor wonders what she will think when the rains come and the summer greens replace the monochrome straw.

The Lukhele family is outside their home as a welcoming party when Lefa and Doctor arrive. The women ululate joyously to welcome Lefa. Tears and laughter mix. Lefa is swallowed into the family of her menfolk. They go inside where Funi has transformed the groceries, that Doctor bought the previous day, into a feast.

After supper, Lefa and Funi share stories of their respective lover and brother; still very much alive in their imaginations. Doctor listens as the picture of his unmet father is given added depth and colour. Long before he left for the City of Gold, he was exploring the veld around KaBokweni. Funi recalls the time when he and a school friend had set off to climb the Legogote mountain.

*

The two boys had estimated the mountain must be about a one-hour hike and then maybe another two hours to make the summit. Nobody in KaBokweni walked just for the sake of it, so a better estimate was not available. They set off just after sunrise expecting to be home mid-afternoon. By mid-morning they had been walking for four hours and the mountain appeared no closer. There was no obvious road in the right direction and the cross-country terrain was difficult; as much up and down as progress towards the horizon. They stopped at a farmhouse and the maid there offered them water and some fresh Portuguese bread. She thought it would take them at least another hour to reach the Petra Mountain Inn which she knew was at the foot of the mountain. They set off again and made good progress so that they were at the Inn around lunchtime. One of the gardeners greeted them as they approached. He smiled as the two lads told him about their day so far and their plan to get to the Lion's Head summit. He pointed them in the direction of the trail head and they set off. A few minutes later the gardener caught them up and handed over some cold Malva pudding that he had persuaded the kitchen staff to give him. The pudding was deliciously sticky and sweet and not something they were used to eating. The march and final scramble to the summit was easy on their now full stomachs. Near the top, they came across a wide cave entrance. Inside, on the cave walls, they discovered some faded drawings of animals; reddish brown buck and a rhinoceros as well as some black, stick herdsmen. The animals were drawn in great detail whereas the humans were just simple representations. Were the animals more interesting to the artists than the people they wondered? They speculated on who might have drawn them but they would have been amazed by the truth. Funi discovered years later that they were believed to be thousands of years old and the work of Khoisan bushmen that were here before any of the rainbow people that now called the Lowveld home and argued about the chronology of their ancestors' arrivals.

From the top of Legogote, the two boys could look east towards the plain that is the southern end of the Kruger National Park and, beyond that, the north-south ridge of the Lebombo Mountains that form the border with Mozambique. To the west, they could see the escarpment above Sabie where wood smoke was rising from the invisible town. They tried to see their own KaBokweni to the south but it was lost in the hazy landscape. For the first time in their lives they could see beyond their small world. Here no policeman was taking an unnecessary interest in their movements. The air was clean and Doctor had a sense of freedom he had not felt before.

On the way down, a green mamba slithered away from its sunbathing rock. It was gone before they had time to be scared.

The Malva Pudding Gardener had finished work and was about to walk home when the boys reappeared. They could not make it home before dark. Malva suggested they stayed with his family overnight and they could leave for home first thing in the morning. The boys were unhappy that their families would be worried but there was no way of contacting them in those days. They did not relish the idea of a long walk in the dark.

Doctor and his friend passed the evening as the guests of Malva, his wife and his mother-in-law. They shared the precious food that they had and the boys slept on the floor with blankets for warmth. Early the next morning they left and they were back in KaBokweni in time for a late breakfast and to the evident relief of their families.

*

Funi is sure that Doctor's curiosity about the world which he had shown from an early age then became a burning desire to escape beyond the horizons he had seen from the top of Legogote mountain.

Lefa adds to the complexity of the sleeping arrangements but she is happy to join Funi in her bed. The two women have already formed a friendship based on their mutual love for the older Doctor who had little time to develop character flaws that might have tempered their feelings for him.

After breakfast, Lefa and her son drive to the shopping mall in Hazyview. The mall is quite new and has brought the copy-paste selection of department stores, supermarkets, international brands and fast food to a rural population for whom a trip to the malls of Mbombela was often unaffordable. The hulking, concrete and clad exterior is ugly but the inside is cool and enticing. Doctor buys his mother some new church shoes which she is very happy about. They are returning to the car when Doctor spots the black Audi with the giveaway plates. Lucas Nozulu parks and he and an elegantly dressed woman, presumably his wife, head into the mall. Doctor hustles Lefa back to the car and leaves her while he turns to follow Nozulu.

Nozulu and his wife separate soon after entering the mall. Nozulu heads for a coffee shop and is shortly joined at his table by two men. Doctor watches them for several minutes as they order coffee and start a lively discussion with some loud laughter that draws attention from the customers close by. The three men seem unperturbed. One of the two men with Nozulu hand him a large envelope, there is a shaking of hands and then they both get up to leave. The coffee arrives but they are already gone. Nozulu folds and stuffs the envelope into the inside pocket of his jacket and nonchalantly sips his coffee.

Doctor returns to his mother and spots the two men getting into a Land Cruiser with Mozambique plates.

Lefa and Doctor drive quietly back to KaBokweni. She is happy simply to be enjoying the company of her son while he is speculating on the meaning of the envelope exchange. There seems little doubt now that there is something very wrong with Lucas Nozulu.

27

That evening, the Lukhele family are again treated to memories of Doctor's father. Lefa recalls the time just after they met when the young couple spent a Sunday afternoon together. They decided to take the short bus ride from Alex to the Zoo Lake in northern Johannesburg. It was early winter and the immigrant Planes around the Lake had already lost their leaves. The Zoo Lake was unusual in those days in that there was free access for all races, a legacy of the Deed of Gift that stipulated the park was for the use of all Johannesburg's citizens. Lefa and the late Doctor bought some roasted mealie and spread a blanket on the grass to enjoy the sunshine and to get close to each other. They had been relaxing for no more than a few minutes when they were approached by a white man and his wife. The man turned out to be one of the researchers at Doctor's workplace. They greeted. Doctor was taken aback. It was very unusual to meet whites outside of a work situation and even more unusual for them to take the lead in greeting. The researcher was Doctor Chris MacDonald and his wife was Helen. They sat on the dry grass close to the blanket and exchanged small talk for a few minutes. They were interested to know more about Lefa who looked extraordinarily pretty in her Sunday clothes. Whites were more accustomed to seeing their black countrymen in tattered, unflattering work clothes and this close-up view of a beautiful Zulu woman was making an impression.

Chris MacDonald mentioned that he had been fighting the previous year with the Defence Force against the Cubans in Angola. Doctor really had no clue about it but Chris went on to say that he was worried for the future of South Africa. Doctor mumbled a few words to the effect that he did not expect much change in his lot in his lifetime. Chris was not so sure. Then his tone became altogether more serious when he asked Doctor if he was interested in the struggle. Doctor was non-committal. He was not about to discuss his attendance at the weekly ANC meetings with a white man that he barely knew. But was it possible that this white man was a sympathiser? More likely he was a spy but Doctor could not imagine that his, so far, petty activism would be of interest to anyone.

They noticed a policeman watching them from fifty yards away and Chris and his wife decided to make their goodbyes and continue their Sunday afternoon walk. The policeman moved towards Doctor and Lefa and asked them brusquely for their pass books. The pass books were duly inspected and the policeman suggested, firmly, they pack up and get themselves back to Alex quickly.

That might have been the end of the story if it had not been for the surprise intervention of a young black man who came from nowhere and started to harangue the policeman. What right did he have to harass two peaceable citizens enjoying their rest day? The policeman pulled his sjambok and lunged at the stranger. Two other SAP appeared and ran towards the fracas. Doctor put his arms around the angry man and dragged him backwards urging him not to get into a fight. A stand-off ensued and eventually the three policemen turned away, laughing.

The stranger introduced himself as Junior. He was still fuming. Once he had calmed down he explained he had been following the white couple that had spoken to them. Junior was with the ANC and MacDonald had been making enquiries through a professor at Wits University who was a known ANC sympathiser. Junior had been tasked with finding out a bit more about this white man who was in the Defence Force Reserve and who benefited from all the advantages of white supremacist rule. The ANC leadership was suspicious of anyone who came forward with the idea of joining the struggle. They preferred to recruit from the huge pool of poorly educated and susceptible youth who were unlikely already to have been recruited by the security forces. Doctor retold the brief conversation they had shared and Junior moved to leave them. He thanked them for holding him back. Probably he would be in the dreaded John Vorster Square by now without them.

Next day, when Doctor saw Chris in the laboratory in Smit Street, there was no acknowledgement of the previous afternoon's encounter or the impression Lefa had made. Chris just bantered with Doctor as always; mildly patronising but completely normal. The struggle was on hold.

*

It is Sunday morning and the extended Lukhele family attends church. Funi proudly introduces her nephew and his new shoes mother to her friends. The mostly Swazi congregation are instantly under the spell of this fine Zulu woman who has brought up the outstanding Doctor, son of their local hero, also Doctor. A pretty young woman with a good singing voice is more deeply spellbound by this living Doctor. She decides she will find a way of getting to know the handsome newcomer and she intercepts Bongile on the way out.

After Church, Lefa and Doctor walk with Funi to the cemetery at the edge of the township. Funi takes the lead and guides them to a grave with a simple sandstone headstone and a stark summary of a short life.

"Doctor Lukhele,
born 3rd October 1958, died 23rd June 1976.
RIP".

Lefa drops to her knees next to the grave and sobs uncontrollably. Doctor kneels beside her and puts his arms around her shaking shoulders. He cannot remember ever seeing her like this. Suddenly she seems small and frail. All through his childhood, she was steely in her resolve to raise him. She had no time for tears and never showed any self-pity despite the hardships she endured and the sacrifices she made. She was endlessly warm and loving towards him and a lioness when it came to protecting him from the risks of adolescence in Soweto. This new side of his mother makes his heart ache. Over the years, he has been curious about his father without ever really missing him. Now he does. He so wishes that his mother had her man to protect her as she ages. Then he realizes the obvious. He is that man. Lefa is grieving for the dead Doctor's wasted life not for herself nor for their uncertain, unlived life together. He renews a silent vow to make her life as comfortable as possible and to assuage the loneliness that she will inevitably experience in years to come.

Funi leads the three of them in a prayer for her brother. Doctor fixes his eyes on his father's headstone and notices a small lizard sunning itself on the top edge. The lizard cocks its heads and stares at him as if challenging him to a game of who blinks first. The late winter sun is at its zenith and the family retire to the shade of Funi's home.

Lefa leaves early on Monday to return to her familiar Highveld. The weekend has passed all too quickly. Doctor drives her into White River to catch the minibus back to Johannesburg. They are both comfortable in a warm silence. Her steel has returned and she hugs him hard, shedding no tears, before taking her seat. He promises to see her soon.

Chapter 6
Abduction

Doctor returns to his wi-fi coffee shop in Mbombela and makes plans for the next few days. He starts by calling Joy. She does not sound very friendly and is reluctant to meet him again. Eventually though she agrees to lunch but insists that it is not in the same coffee shop.

Yesterday's Sunday Times is still available for customers to read and Doctor checks out his article. The story is about a head teacher in a South Johannesburg school who had been using school funds to fund lavish vacation trips for several years. Several of the school's governors were also implicated. Overnight, he has received several Facebook messages praising his investigation. One message, though, is quite vitriolic and threatening. He has received several abusive messages on his twitter account.

Doctor is not so easily frightened. He thinks back to his youth in Soweto. Although his Mother had always been protective of him and ensured that he studied hard, she had not been able to watch his every move. The group of friends that he would hang around with, after school and until his mother came home from work, were no angels. He experienced a growth spurt when he was twelve and thereafter was always physically imposing, tall and muscular. He was often on the fringe of, could not avoid, the brutal violence that permeated the townships after Madiba's release. He witnessed more than one necklacing of accused police informers who were often just guilty of being from the wrong tribe. Several times, he had to dodge rubber bullets as he joined in stone throwing designed to make the area a no-go zone for the police that it targeted.

One afternoon, he was walking home from school with a group of friends when they were confronted by half a dozen youths who were probably a couple of years older. The smart school uniforms that they were wearing, and which their families could barely afford, attracted the youths' unwelcome attention. They started by taunting the friends from a distance, making lude insinuations about their sexuality. Then they picked out the smallest of the group and made a grab for him. He was brought to the ground and the youths tore at his clothing, throwing his shoes into a drain. Doctor hesitated for a moment and then ran to his friend's aid. The rest of the group followed him. Doctor lunged wildly at one of the attackers and received several poorly aimed punches to the body in return. Doctor's counter gave the boy on the ground enough time to get up and run towards the relative safety of a spaza shop. The attackers lost interest and wandered away leaving the friends to regroup and dust themselves down. There were similar incidents happening in the area every day and the outcomes were often more serious. Policing was defensive and the acrid smell of anarchy hung everywhere in the impoverished township.

*

Just after noon, Joy arrives at the little, open-air restaurant in the Botanical Gardens. Doctor is already there. She is more relaxed than she sounded on the phone and even manages a smile. They both order fish and chips. Doctor runs over what he has found. Joy lets out an elongated eish intermittently. Then she mentions that she might know the names of the men from Mozambique. Doctor

34

hands her his note book and a pen and she writes down the two names.

Joy explains that there has recently been a tender for the construction of an irrigation scheme at an agricultural research centre which was awarded to a South African company owned by the two men from Mozambique. She would normally not have sight of such details but a colleague in another department had mentioned it because she was disappointed to see foreigners getting the contract. She adds the name of the company to the names already in the notebook.

Eating less than half of her lunch, Joy makes her excuses and hurries off.

Doctor calls Abu who promises to make another trip to CIPRO. Then he googles local irrigation contractors. He calls three before he finds what he is looking for. He agrees to a meeting in Komatipoort at three that afternoon.

The drive to Komatipoort follows the Crocodile River first through a deep gorge and then out onto a flat landscape of sugar cane plantations. The Lebombo ridge that marks the border with Mozambique is the only feature on the horizon. There is no winter in this border town. It is hot and dusty; parched and awaiting the slaking summer rain. Doctor pulls up in front of the small office and equipment-cluttered yard of Impala Irrigation Pty..

A tall Afrikaner in khaki shirt and shorts comes out of the office and greets Doctor with the traditional African handshake. He introduces himself as Charl and invites Doctor in and offers rooibos tea. Doctor accepts and explains that he is investigating a case of potential corruption. What does he know about the Maputo guys that have just won the contract which Impala was hopeful of getting?

Charl says he had never heard of them until the contract was awarded. He thinks this is odd because he knows everyone in the business around here. But he can only shrug and decide to sharpen his pencil next time a tender comes in. Still, he thinks he was pretty competitive and is struggling to see how the new competition could have undercut him. Another thing that strikes him as odd is that the Mozambicans got the contract even though their company does not have the black economic empowerment rating specified in the tender document.

Doctor thanks Charl and returns to his car. On the drive, back to KaBokweni, Doctor takes stock of his investigation. At some point, he needs to confront Nozulu but it is too early and he is fairly sure that he has yet to fully appreciate the extent of his corruption. He needs to try to get to April Coetzee. He pulls into a layby overlooking the Crocodile River, cascading around and over sandstone boulders a hundred metres below the road. He calls the switchboard at the Provincial Administration and asks for Mrs. Coetzee. He gets through to her assistant. Coetzee is in a meeting but her assistant takes a message and promises she will call back.

Several times during the day, Doctor has noticed a large Toyota bakkie in his rear-view mirror. It is never very close so it is not easy to be sure it is the same vehicle. Now he decides that it is not paranoid to conclude it is and that it is following him.

As he approaches Mbombela with the setting sun dazzling him, Doctor picks up to hear the irritated tones of April Coetzee. What does he want? Doctor explains that he needs to meet her. She is reluctant but they agree to meet in an hour at Doctor's favourite coffee shop.

April Coetzee is on time. Doctor is already nursing a passionfruit and lemonade. She has no difficulty spotting him and approaches. She looks confident and business like in a knee-length dress and understated jewellery. Her hair is tied back giving her face a severe look at odds with the relaxed visage he had noted when she swept passed him at the guest house.

Doctor wastes no time coming to the point. He is convinced that her boss is involved in corrupt practices and he is pretty sure she is implicated too but probably just a small part of a much bigger story. What does she know about his links with the Mozambicans? If she can help him, maybe she can avoid the big hole that Nozulu is about to be swallowed by. April smiles nervously and asks what help she can offer. Doctor needs to know everything she knows. April seems to agree but she says that this is not the place or the time. She suggests they meet later that evening at her home. Doctor suspects this is a trap and wonders why they do not just talk further in her car.

April leaves and Doctor settles the bill and follows her out. It is now dark but her car is easy to spot, just fifty metres away. He walks towards the Range Rover but is still several paces away when he is felled by a blow to the head.

Doctor recovers consciousness and takes in the sound of tree frogs and a cacophony of goggas. His arms are tied behind his back and it is completely dark. He guesses he is in the boot of a car; his feet are also bound and he is unable to stretch without hitting the sides. His head aches from the blow. He experiences a flashback to his father's fatal interrogation which his imagination has rehearsed many times before but without the added frisson of his current situation. He is very frightened.

After a few minutes that seem much longer, he hears a vehicle approaching. Then the boot opens and he is not sure whether to be surprised to see April Coetzee and then Lucas Nozulu looking at him, dazzling him with their flashlight. The big man cuts the plastic binding around his feet and helps him into a sitting position.

Nozulu announces that Doctor is a very lucky man. Doctor is at first puzzled and the explanation that follows is not what he is expecting.

Nozulu explains that he had been in the back of his colleague's car waiting for him to join her outside the coffee shop. They had watched as a man had run up behind him and hit him with what looked like a crowbar.

They had seen him bundled, unconscious, into the boot of his own Polo. The attacker had found the car keys and driven off. Coetzee had no difficulty following in her Range Rover. The Polo and its unconscious owner had been driven for twenty kilometres or so west on the main highway towards Johannesburg. She had followed at a discreet distance until it turned off on a sand road. She parked the Range Rover off-road and waited with Nozulu still in the back seat.

A few minutes later, a powerful bakkie with Gauteng plates pulled onto the highway from the sand road. Nozulu moved into the seat next to Coetzee and pulled the 9mm pistol he always carried.

38

They nosed cautiously down the sand road for a couple of kilometres before spotting the Polo. It had been driven off the road until it had grounded on a rock. The attacker was nowhere to be seen and they guessed he was probably already 20 kilometres away in the bakkie they had seen.

The Polo's keys were not in the ignition but they were able to open the boot using the lever alongside the driver's seat.

Doctor is not sure that he believes this story which puts him in the uncomfortable position of needing to be grateful to the two probable crooks that he has been investigating. Who had attacked him if not these two or their accomplices? His still befuddled head starts to clear and he remembers the threatening tweets following his Sunday Times article of the weekend.

Doctor tries an overly casual thankyou and asks Nozulu to release his bound hands. Nozulu is in no hurry. Doctor is planning to publish allegations which threaten to destroy his career and put an end to his wealth creating schemes. Nozulu reasons he may never have a better chance to eliminate the threat. But he is not a killer. He has never fired the 9mm pistol. Coetzee is following his train of thoughts. She is regretting her involvement in this whole thing forgetting that she is, in fact, instrumental.

Nozulu makes a suggestion; he can help Doctor with a much bigger story in return for a little forgetfulness and his promise to curtail the graft which has been central to his life for a few years already. Doctor is sceptical but plays along. Actually, Doctor has decided that Nozulu is unlikely to do him harm. Why bother to follow his kidnappers rather than leave him to his fate?

For the moment, the three of them agree to a truce in the interests of getting home and getting some sleep. Nozulu cuts the binding around Doctor's wrists and he manages to get himself out of the boot.

Doctor has the benefits of a free Soweto education as well as his expensive varsity training. The former enables him to hotwire the ignition on his keyless car. Being fifteen years old, the Polo is not endowed with the security features that would probably frustrate him if it were a more recent model. It starts immediately. Pushing the car off the rock on which it is stranded, Doctor drives the yards back to the sand road and point it towards the highway. The Range Rover draws alongside and a meeting in the afternoon of the new day, at the guest house, is agreed through open windows.

The smart SUV roars off leaving a cloud of dust in the Polo's headlights. Doctor follows more slowly, just thankful to be alive.

It is the early hours of the morning when Doctor makes it back to KaBokweni. Funi, awakened by his car, meets him at the door. She tuts and clucks her concern seeing that he is dishevelled from his ordeal. There is congealed blood from the blow on his head but otherwise he seems to be in reasonable shape. He tells his aunt that he suspects his article in the Sunday Times has provoked the attack. He does not go into the detail, his abduction and rescue by the subjects of his current investigation. Funi seems satisfied with the bare bones and is just pleased to have her nephew back in more or less one piece.

Doctor wakes late the following morning. He has a splitting headache. The house is empty.

As he is making tea, there is a hello and a knock at the front door. It is a young woman. He vaguely remembers her face from church last Sunday. It looks like she is wearing her Church dress. She has a pretty, open face and fixes her brown eyes on him in a quite disconcerting way. She explains that Bongile had called her this morning and told her briefly about his violent experience of the previous evening. Her name is Hlengiwe. Can she help? Doctor recovers his poise a little and explains that he is fine and is planning on leaving shortly and heading to Mbombela. They share his sweet tea; strangely intimate for two people that have just met he thinks. Hlengiwe mentions she needs to pick up her Golf after its service.

Doctor hot wires his Polo and opens the passenger door for Hlengiwe. They drive quietly into White River and its new, all glass, VW dealer. Hlengiwe bids him farewell but not before leaving Doctor her phone number and extracting a promise that they will meet again soon. She is experienced enough in these matters to know that Doctor is smitten and her first impressions from a distance in the Church are confirmed on closer inspection although maybe he is a bit older than she had thought. She is particularly impressed by his gentle, confident way of speaking.

Doctor remembers his lost key and heads for the spares department. The woman that greets him is able to order a new ignition key for his Polo and promises to call him when it arrives.

Chapter 7
The Minister

The minister is sitting in his elegant office in the Union Building in Pretoria. He is wearing an expensive suit which fits him perfectly. He is catching up with the weekend's Sunday Times which had lain unread at his Sandton home while he was on the golf course. He had had a good day; bettering his handicap of twelve by several shots.

An article on page three, exposing corruption in the Johannesburg school system, has caught his eye. Reports like this are irksome but, in a way, he thinks, they are helpful in keeping peoples' minds off the bigger picture. As this thought crosses his mind, he is momentarily ashamed of his cynicism but the devil in his other ear soon restores normal service and an involuntary smirk forms on his lips.

The article is credited to Doctor Lukhele. The name rings a bell but he cannot think why. He googles the name to find that it belongs to a freelance reporter who cannot have been born in the distant past that he is trying to recall.

His secretary enters the office with his morning coffee and a croissant. She reminds him that the first of several meetings is due to start in five minutes. His renewed attempt to dredge up the memory that is nagging deep in the archives of his mind is interrupted for a second time by the sound of an incoming WhatsApp message from his mistress, chiding him for failing to turn up for a date the previous evening which he had spent with his golfing friends and a bottle of very good malt whisky.

Then Junior Khumalo's day starts in earnest and his attempt to make the connection with Doctor is forgotten.

Chapter 8
Arrests

Doctor heads for the Guest House on the Plaston Road. It is too early for his meeting with Nozulu and Coetzee but he is hoping to speak to the owner on her own if possible. As he approaches the turning into the Guest House driveway he notices a cluster of blue flashing lights. He drives past slowly trying to work out what is happening. There are several police cars in the guest house car park and a lot of activity. A Range Rover is also in the car park. Doctor accelerates away from the scene. He has a bad feeling about the likely reason for the activity.

The bad feeling is confirmed a few hours later when Doctor tunes into the radio news which is headlined by the discovery of the body of a white woman in a room at the Guest House.

A further hour passes and the news confirms that the body is April Coetzee and that she has been shot.

Doctor calls Joy who is in quite a state. She volunteers that Lucas Nozulu is not in the office although his car is still parked in the staff car park where it seems it has been since the previous day. The police are at the offices and asking questions. She also mentions that she has some new information which she will send him by e-mail.

Next Doctor calls Abu. He has news from his latest visit to CIPRO. The company that won the irrigation tender is owned by the two Mozambicans that Joy had named when they met at the Botanical Gardens. Even more interesting is the discovery that Mrs. Pardon Nozulu is also a Director.

Doctor drives back to KaBokweni in the late afternoon. As he pulls into his aunt's yard, two police cars block the entrance. He is under arrest and a suspect in the murder of April Coetzee. Bongile rushes out of the home and sees him bundled into the back of one of the police cars in handcuffs. There is no chance to ask any questions or to find out where Doctor is being taken.

Doctor is driven to Mbombela and locked into a stark, brightly lit cell in the police station in the centre of town. His smart phone and wallet are taken from him.

Doctor is dazed and confused after the fast-moving events of the last 24 hours. He absorbs the sterile atmosphere of his cell and again finds himself thinking about the last few weeks of his father's life.

His mother had told him what she knew from the time she met his father until his death in prison later that year. He had filled in the considerable gaps with knowledge he had gained while researching the rise and fall of Apartheid and before he fell under the spell of alcohol.

Doctor's research had started with his father's dog-eared pass book which his mother had kept. The senior Doctor had been arrested in the winter of 1976 during a protest in Soweto, a few days after the tumultuous June 16th uprising. The fact that he was obviously not carrying his passbook must have made his arrest and detention more certain.

The battered, brown "dompas" contained a black and white photograph of a glum but handsome sixteen-year-old Doctor

Lukhele and confirmed his Swazi ancestry. On another of the indexed pages his employment record showed that he had started work in Johannesburg in April 1975 at the National Institute for Metallurgy in Smit Street. He was still there, spending his days washing laboratory glassware, at the time of the final entry in June 1976.

In the evenings, his father took an ochre PUTCO bus to Alexandra township ten miles north of his workplace where he shared a room in a bleak hostel with several other young men. He would club together with his roommates to buy chicken stew and mieliepap from an impromptu kitchen set up on First Street. He slept badly, covered by a single blanket which leaked his precious body heat every time he turned over. On Sundays, Doctor would put on his second-hand suit and go to St Hubert's church.

Doctor had recently met Lefa, after Church, while the congregation mingled over the free tea and Marie biscuits that were consumed enthusiastically as a reward for attending. She was a pretty Zulu woman who had been born in Alex. Lefa was working with an Indian shopkeeper who ran a haberdashery in Fordsburg. Like most young black people, her childhood had been short and impoverished but she was now enjoying having a little money of her own even though she knew that her education had ended too soon for her to test her potential. Lefa was struck by Doctor's quiet and thoughtful nature that seemed to suggest a character that already had depth and would develop further. He was also very good looking and well put together.

The hostel was a fertile nursery for the ANC and their local leaders held meetings every Wednesday evening which were well attended by the hostel's inhabitants. Life was not easy for the banned ANC and the Black Consciousness Movement was more active in Alex at that time. Nevertheless, the ANC was tightening its grip, particularly on young people of Doctor's age. During the meetings, bulletins were read out from the ANC leadership in exile. Usually these included dry diatribes about diplomatic contacts with sympathising countries who in turn were using their channels to exhort the Apartheid regime to take a softer stance. There were accounts of life in training camps in Angola. Sometimes there would be a verbal update on an act of sabotage carried out by uMkhonto weSizwe, the ANC's armed wing. A water main on the East Rand had been ruptured by a bomb in May but such excitement was rare. The generation of the Rivonia Treason Trial was already aging and its energies were focused on mostly on civil disobedience and gaining support overseas. It would take a new upheaval to mobilize the younger generation. In recent weeks, the bulletins had become much more immediate and focused on the growing unrest in Soweto and other large black townships around the issue of compulsory teaching in the Afrikaans language for key subjects. Members were encouraged to organise and participate in protests and to support students taking part in strikes.

Doctor attended the meetings initially because it was a break from the winter evening tedium and for the tea and the still warm, deep fried magwinya that were served. Occasionally, he would pick up a discarded copy of the New Age in the hostel common room. He found himself gradually warming to the possibility that it was not inevitable that black people would always be subjugated by their white countrymen. Ironically, he spoke Afrikaans almost fluently; growing up in the Lowveld meant regular contact with Afrikaner farmers and officials, and some of his basic education had been taught in the language. He also spoke SiSwati and Zulu and his English had improved rapidly since his arrival in Johannesburg. In other circumstances his talent for languages would have been noted and encouraged. Here it was mainly about survival.

The Wednesday morning of the sixteenth June dawned bitterly cold. Doctor caught the bus into the Johannesburg CBD at six and by seven thirty he was donning his white laboratory coat which he imagined made him, with one important difference, look like the research officers that he worked close to and who bantered light heartedly with him during the day when he would regularly visit their benches to collect the dirty glassware from the experiments that were running.

During the day, Doctor became aware of a buzz and sense of disquiet growing amongst his white colleagues. The woman that manned the tea trolley in the canteen told him that she had heard there had been some trouble in Soweto but she did not have any details. She had a transistor radio in the kitchen and the two of them huddled close to it to listen to the crackly news at three pm. The bulletin was sketchy but it spoke of student protestors killing a police dog, throwing stones at the police in Orlando West and setting fire to police cars and public buildings.

On the bus home, a fellow passenger spoke of the protests in Soweto and that he had heard that several protesters had been shot by the police.

At the meeting that evening, the ANC leader confirmed that two students had been killed by police during the day's protests. There was shock then anger in the room. The protestors had apparently been running away when the shots were fired. It was announced that there would be a "stay away" on Friday and a protest in Soweto on Saturday afternoon. Buses would be laid on to take people who wanted to join the protest.

Doctor did not stay away from work on the Friday. He was still doubtful that such action could make any difference and anyway he was worried that he would lose his job and be forced to return to his family in the Lowveld of Eastern Transvaal. He was slightly abashed when he met Lefa that evening and learnt that she had not been to the haberdashery and had in fact joined a protest in Alex which clashed with the police that afternoon. Her eyes were red and swollen from the teargas. She needed his strong and reassuring body in a very pleasing way that night.

Saturday was another crisp, blindingly blue, Highveld winter day but by the time the buses arrived in Alex it was quite warm. About a hundred, mostly young, men and women boarded the buses. Doctor settled into a well-worn seat near the back of the second bus in the convoy which headed south for Soweto passing close to the carefully tended gardens of the white suburbs and his downtown workplace on Smit Street. For Doctor, the trip had the feeling of a Church outing; a welcome break from the monotony of everyday life tinged with the excitement of what the day might have in store.

The buses were soon rolling across the dry veld that separated the city from the southern townships. They passed rocky kopjes and signs that suggested Bloemfontein could be reached for a late lunch if you were the oblivious white family in their Austin Apache saloon that Doctor glimpsed as they overtook. They were from another world, Doctor thought.

As the buses approached Soweto, they were confronted by a police road block. Several SAPs with dogs boarded the bus and scanned the passengers who were mostly too frightened to be angry. Doctor had left his passbook at Lefa's place when he left her in the early hours and he was sure that he would be arrested if he was unable to produce it. Instead the SAPs told the driver to turn back and, apparently disinterested, they got off after administering a gratuitous slap around the head to each of two belligerently muttering youths in the front seats.

The bus turned back towards Johannesburg but the same youths that had attracted the attention of the cops earlier now forced the driver to stop as soon as they were well clear of the road block. Without any obvious instructions, the whole busload disembarked and started to run across the winter straw veld towards Diepkloof. The air was scented and stained with wood smoke from the township home fires.

The group jogged for quite a time into the regimented streets and apparently deserted housing of Diepkloof. They could see smoke rising ahead of them and they emerged from the township into an open area around Orlando stadium. Here there were hundreds of protestors and beyond them a line of police and dogs. Over the din of the crowd, he could hear the chatter of a helicopter. Doctor had never encountered tear gas but he knew immediately that it was in the acrid air and that it was what he could taste in his mouth. An armoured car spraying its water cannon came towards the crowd and Doctor was knocked off his feet by the force of the water. The armoured car stopped and four or five armed cops jumped out and started to shambok anybody within reach. Doctor received a couple of kicks in the ribs and a blow to the head from one of them; a black. Doctor briefly locked eyes with him and he understood that this man was as frightened as he was. The black policeman was joined by a couple of his white colleagues; both only a little older than Doctor. The three of them grabbed Doctor's arms and one leg and carried him awkwardly, writhing uselessly, towards the armoured car. He felt oddly detached from the chaos around him and the confusion of noises became tinny and distant as if he was hearing a recording. They threw him in the back with several other bleeding protestors and the detachment evaporated as the doors were slammed shut and locked. The armoured car drove off at speed hurling the already bruised occupants against each other and the sides of the vehicle. A few minutes later they lurched to a halt and the rear doors opened. Doctor and his fellow prisoners were ordered to get out, only to be momentarily blinded by the afternoon sun. Doctor found himself stood, shivering and smeared with somebody else's blood, in a yard behind a police station. Several Alsatian police dogs pulled on their leads and snarled threateningly at the pathetic group. They were marched inside. Doctor and six others were locked into a cell comfortably big enough for three people.

Doctor stayed in the cell for three nights by which time it was a stinking hell and literally freezing at night. If he could have moved he would have realized that his joints had stiffened with the cold. He was weak with thirst and hunger; he had eaten nothing since breakfast on Saturday.

While enduring the long hours in the overcrowded cell, Doctor had got talking to a Zulu man of his age. They shared stories of their childhood and found ways to joke about their current dilemma. Without understanding why, Doctor asked his cell mate to look after a photograph of his mother and younger sister, Funi, which he carried everywhere.

51

On the third morning, the cell door was opened and Doctor found himself pulled out and marched to a small room with a table and two chairs. A young cop, staring but silent, placed an enamel mug of weak tea in front of him. Reviving a little, Doctor realized that his clothes were soiled and that he badly needed a shower. This did not seem to be a problem for the thick set, middle-aged Afrikaner who entered the room and sat opposite him. They sat silently looking at each other for several minutes. Doctor was surprised to see the same fearful eyes that he had seen in the black policeman on Saturday. The man removed his jacket and started his interrogation. Doctor reasoned that he had nothing to hide. He had hardly had time to realize that he was actually involved in a protest before his arrest. Surely, he would be released soon and surely simply telling his story would speed up his release. He was worried about how he was going to get home in his current state. He expected he would be in trouble at work too. He answered the Afrikaner's questions easily in a mix of Afrikaans and English. He began to worry more when the policeman asked him repeatedly to explain why he did not have his passbook. He seemed convinced this was an act of defiance rather than just sleepy neglect. The Afrikaner seemed to be more than just a little interested in the fact that he was Swazi and that his mother tongue was SiSwati. There were not so many Swazi's in Jo'burg. Why did he think he must have spent some time in Mozambique? How could he know that he was a regular at the Wednesday evening meetings in his hostel? The interview now got more difficult when he was asked for the names of his friends who attended the meetings. Up to this point the interview had been terse but not unfriendly. Now the Afrikaner got angry.

Doctor recovered consciousness some time later. He was lying on a cold floor and he moved tentatively before feeling his ribs. He was in pain. Every part of his body was stiff and sensitive to the touch. There was a sticky patch in his hair which proved to be dry blood. This time, it was his blood. Looking around and getting accustomed to the darkness he learnt that he was in a cell alone. He had an instinct that he was no longer in the Soweto police station but there were no windows so it was impossible to say.

A plate of gristly meat stew and mashed squash was pushed under the cell door. Doctor wolfed it down and felt almost human for a while.

The next day or maybe it was the night; Doctor was woken from a fitful sleep by two policemen who hauled him roughly to a new interrogation room. There was a man in the shadows of the poorly lit room. He stepped forward and Doctor recognised the Afrikaner that had beaten him up. As he approached, Doctor fixed his interrogator's stare. Again, that now familiar fear looked back at him.

The Afrikaner was to be the last person on earth that Doctor would talk to. It was not a long conversation.

Lefa was worried when Doctor did not attend Church on Sunday morning. She knew he had planned to go to the protest in Soweto and there was a rumour circulating in the congregation that a number of Alex boys had been arrested the previous afternoon.

The rumour was confirmed but Doctor did not re-appear when the Alex boys were released a few days later. Doctor's beaten body was already on its way to KaBokweni and his distraught family who had been told that he had hanged himself in his cell.

Lefa could only guess, fearfully, at the fate that had befallen the Doctor that she was just beginning to love. She attended the ANC meeting at his hostel on the following Wednesday and one of the leaders promised to make enquiries.

Several days later, the ANC man visited Lefa in the haberdashery shop. He had learnt that Doctor had died in custody and he was matter of fact in giving her the news. He mentioned that the police were saying he had hanged himself but that it was more likely he had died under interrogation. He was sorry.

Lefa did not know how to react. She had not known Doctor for long enough to have forgotten how to live without him but she knew he was special to her and the news of his death had created an agonising ache in the pit of her stomach. She tried to pull herself together before returning to the shop counter. Her boss, seeing her distress, sent her home.

Lefa spent the next few weeks in a state of confusion and anger. The unrest continued into the Spring and her Doctor was not the first or the last casualty. The ANC drew energy from the police brutality waged on their people. Young men of Doctor's age began leaving. Rumours suggested they were travelling north to Zambia and the ANC training camps there.

By mid-September, Lefa was sure that she was pregnant. Her parents were especially unhappy that she could not produce the father. Nevertheless, they supported her and the junior Doctor was born into a poor but secure home in March.

It is not the first time, of course, that junior Doctor has reconstructed the last days of his father's life. He had filled in the gaps with a mixture of facts gleaned from the well documented story of the June uprising and by assuming that the experiences of others could probably help to answer some of the remaining questions. It was not completely satisfactory. Why did his father attract such violent attention? Why was he not simply released like his fellows on the bus? Doctor thought the authorities must have decided he was an infiltrator who had been trained in Mozambique and come to Johannesburg under ANC orders. His home in the Lowveld, near the border, and his Swazi origins would have made this plausible to the paranoid operators in the SAP who knew that they would not be asked to account for the unexplained death of a young black man. The unmet father was most likely on course to be a bit part player in the fight for freedom rather than the hero martyr that he became in return for his lost life.

Back in the present, Doctor's thoughts are interrupted by the opening cell door and a young police officer who escorts him to an interrogation room. Doctor sits on one side of a table on which there is a recording machine. They are joined by a detective. The suspect and interrogator are about the same age. The detective has a slight build and the air of a man in a hurry, perhaps for his

55

next promotion. Doctor sits opposite the detective and endures the awkward silence. Doctor asks when he might expect to be released. The detective has a few questions and then maybe he can go. Doctor asks if he can call a friend and arrange for a lawyer. A phone is brought to him. He calls Abu who promises to get in touch with an attorney he knows in Mbombela. It is now eight in the evening.

The attorney arrives about two hours later and in the meantime Doctor and the young uniformed policeman have occupied the interrogation room in silence except for the offer and acceptance of a cup of strong, sweet tea. Doctor takes in the bare walls, counts the electrical outlets and watches a lizard hunting for insects on the other side of the single window, the bright light from which is his lure.

The attorney is one of Abu's friends, Fatima Merchant. Fatima looks to be about forty and Doctor is struck by her piercing green eyes. She is business-like, even stiff, in her initial approach. She starts by asking Doctor to tell her a bit about himself and gradually she seems to warm to him. They move on to discussing the possible reasons for his arrest. Doctor explains he is investigating some corrupt practices that involve April and her boss, Lucas Nozulu. He describes the events of the previous night and the plan to meet up at the Guest House that afternoon. He cannot imagine why the police suspect him of involvement in the murder but he mentions his earlier visits to the Guest House and the skirmish with the armed response guys which he guesses may have led to his arrest in KaBokweni.

Fatima leaves the interrogation room to talk to the detective and returns a few minutes later. There is no evidence to link Doctor with the crime so he will be released. The police just need to know where Doctor intends to be for the next few days in case they need to speak to him again. Fatima mentions that she has only briefly described the events of the previous night and April's role in them, and that she felt that it was not helpful to go into the details of his investigation.

Doctor retrieves his phone and wallet and thanks Fatima for her help. She leaves him with her phone number in case he needs her again. She drives off leaving him without obvious means to return to KaBokweni that evening. It is past midnight and too late for a bus or a taxi.

As Doctor is walking towards the main road that will lead him to the edge of town and a possible lift home, a car pulls alongside and the passenger side window drops to reveal Lucas Nozulu in the driver's seat. He is alone. Lucas suggests he gets in. Doctor's intuition is still that Lucas does not represent an immediate threat. Indeed, the big man looks to be in a state of some anxiety. Doctor joins him in the car which he observes is not the black Audi. Lucas tells him it is his wife's, as if reading his mind.

Lucas agrees to drive Doctor to KaBokweni and initially they drive in silence. Finally, Doctor asks him what happened. Lucas pulls in on the verge and starts to cry. Pulling himself together, his life is falling apart he says. He and April had met with the Mozambicans in the early hours. Lucas had called them to warn them that their scam had been discovered. The meeting had become heated. A rattled April had told them that she was going to the police. The Mozambicans made it clear, before leaving, that that would be a big mistake. Lucas left with them in the hope of calming them down and reassuring them that he would manage April. They had dropped him outside his home, promising to stay in touch. He had assumed they would head home to Maputo and be at the border when it opened at seven a.m.

When Lucas started to call April around ten that morning, he got only her voicemail. She did not call him back and by the early afternoon it became obvious why. He figured that his Mozambican friends had returned to the Guest House and killed April. Doctor is puzzled. Why did they not also dispose of Lucas who is surely now a major threat and top of the list for the police to interview? He does not share his thoughts with Lucas.

The pair drive silently to KaBokweni and Doctor is greeted by his Aunt behind the locked bars of her front doors as they enter her yard. Lucas drives off, leaving Doctor with his cell number as, for the second time in as many days, Funi acts as mother hen to her dishevelled and exhausted nephew.

Doctor wakes late again. He takes stock of his situation. He decides the threat from the Joburg folk that had taken exception to his Sunday Times exposé of school leadership corruption is no longer his biggest worry. For the moment, they probably think he is lying dead or dying in the back of his abandoned car. For them the damage is done anyway and the police are probably already interviewing the people he has fingered.

More serious though is the possibility that the Mozambicans will come after him and he cannot rule out that Lucas turns nasty when he gets a grip of himself after the seismic disturbance that almost certainly will curtail his lavish lifestyle. Then there are the police who may still feel that he is not above suspicion.

Doctor checks his e-mails and is immediately drawn to one from Joy's personal e-mail account with the promised new information. She describes a payment of fifty million rand made in the last few days to the Mozambicans' Irrigation Company; unusual because no goods or services have so far been provided.

Elsewhere, Lucas is weighing up his options. He could try to bluff his way through the storm that is definitely about to descend on him. He could disappear. The latter option will make him the lead suspect in April's murder and lead to a damning investigation of his professional conduct. He decides he needs to try to maintain as much normality as possible. He tells his wife just the bare minimum of the events of the last two days but enough to make her understand that trouble is imminent and that he may not be around much. She knows very little of her husband's business and extramural affairs but has long realized that her lifestyle is beyond that earned by his salary alone.

Pardon Nozulu drops her husband at the Government Buildings at nine on Wednesday morning. He does his best to look cool but his secretary informs him that the police are waiting for him in his office so the façade is hard to maintain. There are two plain clothes men in his office; one of whom is the ambitious detective of Doctor's brief encounter. He introduces himself as Lungi Pule. His colleague is Hector Marais.   They want to know his movements on the night of April's murder. He decides the best thing is to be as truthful as possible without giving away too much, too soon. He knows Doctor has been interviewed and he has to assume that they have his version of the events of that night. He admits that he was with April and recounts the story of Doctor's abduction and his role in his rescue. The Mozambicans do not figure in his narrative. Pule points out that nothing in his story takes him out of the frame for April's murder. On the contrary, he seems to be the only suspect. Why was he with April that evening after office hours? Why did he leave his car in the staff car park over the last two nights? Where was he in the hours after the murder and how did he get home? What exactly was his relationship with April apart from being her boss. Lucas realizes that the office gossip on this last question would have been shared with the police by now. He admits that he had been having an affair with April.

Lucas leaves his office in handcuffs. The police take him to his home and he hands over the clothes he wore the previous evening. They search his home and take other clothing for testing. Pardon is distressed, confused and then angry at the mess her home is left in. She is also angry because a colleague of her husband has called her and hinted at his possible connection with April and now her murder. She had supposed until now that the police were interested in his business affairs.

Now it is Lucas's turn to study the white walls of his starkly lit, windowless cell.

Doctor spends the morning penning a piece about the murder of April; connecting the murder to allegations of misconduct in her professional life and her relationship with the prime suspect in her murder. He had hoped that he would have more time to build the case but now the murder is headline news he needs to get his story out. He calls the editor at the Sunday Times and gives him an outline of the story. The editor is enthralled and suggests they keep some of the details of his investigation under wraps for another week and aim to publish the story with the initial findings surrounding the guest house payments and its use as an illicit meeting place for Lucas and April. The Mozambicans will perhaps be lured into thinking that their role in the story will remain out of the public eye. In the meantime, Doctor can continue to dig into their affairs. They must assume that Lucas will tell the police about them to ensure that he is not the only suspect.

Doctor finishes his first draft and calls Hlengiwe. She is at work but agrees to meet him in the mall in Mbombela when she finishes later that afternoon.

Chapter 9
Hlengiwe

On the way to her date, Hlengiwe daydreams about her childhood friend, Sipho, who back then, would walk hand in hand with her to their primary school. Sipho was a bright boy with an impish sense of humour which could be annoying but usually just made her laugh even though she wanted to be serious. His father died of AIDS when he was just a toddler and his mother scraped a living selling woodcarvings to tourists on their way to the Kruger Park. In the holidays, they would roast mealies in Sipho's backyard and sell them to passers-by for a couple of rand. When they were 9 years old, Sipho got sick and was away from school more and more often. At school, he had no energy and his cheekiness turned to sullen lethargy. During the Christmas holidays, he got pneumonia and died. Hlengiwe was angry with God; how could He be so unfair. Perhaps this is a factor in her stubborn single status. Is she still reluctant to give her affection away and risk losing the object of that affection?

Hlengiwe arrives at the Greek restaurant. She is wearing a navy business suit, a white shirt, stylish flat shoes and just a pair of pearl studs in her ears; no other jewellery and no make-up. Doctor notices that she is beautiful in a way he had not fully appreciated when they first met. She is tall and slim and walks with the confidence of the first generation of South Africans who are able to benefit fully from the opportunities on offer since the iniquities of the Apartheid system fell away in the last decade of the twentieth century. They both order soft drinks and Hlengiwe slips easily into a description of her day. She is a quantity surveyor and a partner in the business she works in. Her day had included a trip to a construction site in Barberton and she had enjoyed the drive back with the setting sun casting long shadows across the winter landscape of dry, rolling hills and rocky outcrops. Not for the first time, Doctor is self-conscious about his rather scruffy appearance and mentally he is already spending some of the fee he expects for his story on some decent clothes that might help in his courtship of this woman. He has made up his mind that he is going to get to know Hlengiwe.

Hlengiwe moves her hand over Doctor's head to check on the healing gash he had sustained earlier in the week. It has been a long time since a woman other than his Mother had touched him with that kind of tenderness and he realizes he has missed it. He blushes and she laughs.

Continuing easily, Hlengiwe mentions that she still lives with her mother in KaBokweni; her father is late. Excitingly though, she has just bought a townhouse in Mbombela and plans to move in with her Mother in the next month when her purchase completes.

Doctor recounts his part in the last few days and his brush with the law. Normally, he is remarkably confident when he speaks but with her he finds himself strangely tongue-tied and shy. Nevertheless, Hlengiwe is impressed and concerned at the same time. Is he not worried about his safety? To her, the idea of pursuing such an insecure profession and a risky one at that, is foreign. That only adds to the appeal of the man she thinks.

Doctor changes the subject and asks her, tentatively, why she is still single. Her initial reaction, surprise at the question, makes Doctor worry that he has been too bold. Her explanation is quite predictable; she is concentrating on her career and there is a shortage of eligible men in the area. A lot of the boys in her class did not go to varsity; they mostly lacked motivation or their families the funds. She had been determined and her family had managed to scrape together the money needed to top up the bursary she got for achieving good results in her matric. exams. Now the boys had become men mostly without prospects and narrow horizons.

Doctor getting bolder still, suggests that, given her looks, there must nevertheless be a small number of very interested men from whom she could take her pick. Now it is her turn to blush.

Doctor, maybe to atone for being forward, feels it is necessary to explain to her the reason for his soft drink. Maybe he is not so different from the boys in her class he suggests. Hlengiwe seems to be neither surprised nor discouraged. She, in turn, explains her mother suffered for years from the drunken beatings that her father would regularly administer and that she had decided as a girl that she would never drink. Doctor's awareness and obvious determination to fight his addiction only reinforces her positive feelings for him.

The two relax with each other and enjoy their food while talking mostly about the mundane. By the time they get to coffee they have been together for nearly three hours and it is obvious to each of them that the other is reluctant to end the evening. They check out the cinema and choose the late showing of a film that neither is the least bit interested in. The next day neither will even remember its title let alone the story line.

Chapter 10
Lucas Nozulu

Lucas wakes in his cell on Thursday morning and uses the basic but clean facilities to relieve and wash himself. He is deeply depressed. Normally, at this time, he would be preparing to drive to his office and spend his day in meetings with people who wanted only to impress him. Things are about to get worse.

An overweight policeman brings Lucas a breakfast tray with coffee and oats. He is polite but does not linger in the cell; leaving Lucas alone again to fall deeper into his despond.

Lucas reflects on his rise and what now looks like the beginning of his fall.

He remembers his childhood in a small township east of Mbombela (Nelspruit in those days), called Kanyamazane. Now it is a fast-growing community of modest, middle class homes; the new builds are mostly in gated communities or clusters. Then, it was a collection of hastily built block houses with no electricity and just a stand pipe to which he walked each day with his siblings to fill five litre water containers for their home. A spaza shop run by an Indian family sold a few basics; only those few things that the inhabitants could afford. His father had been employed as a gardener and his mother a cleaner in a wealthy home in town where they lived in a cottage in the home's garden. His parents had been forcibly resettled to the township in 1978. They were well treated by their employers and enjoyed job security for many years even after the resettlement. He had attended the township's primary school and then the Cyril Clarke High

School at Mataffin on the edge of Nelspruit, where he achieved good grades in the matric. exams. The school, for black pupils, was funded by local landowners and was the best of its kind in the Eastern Transvaal. His parents could not afford to send him to varsity and he had joined the ANC when it was unbanned in 1990. He rapidly became one of the local party leaders and got a good job in the Provincial Administration after the elections in 1994.

Initially he shadowed an Afrikaner woman who was a buyer in the Purchasing Department. Then he was sent on several short management courses in Johannesburg and proved that he could lead and motivate the small team of buyers that he inherited from another Afrikaner taking early retirement. Three years ago, he had been promoted to head up the department responsible for Agriculture, Rural Development and Land Administration. He was not a particularly ambitious man and the professional success he had seemed to come easily. He did not feel the need to push for even better things. His life was so much better than he had dreamed possible as a schoolboy. Until the arrival of the journalist which had led quickly to April's murder, nobody had ever looked closely at his extramural activities. He realised he had got greedy and complacent. He could think of several critical moments in the last fifteen years when he could have taken a different direction that would certainly not have crossed paths with the tall investigator with his roots in the area that Lucas called home.

*

Some hours later, Lucas is led out of his cell, down a passageway to the same interrogation room that had hosted Doctor earlier. Detective Pule enters and the two men greet cautiously. The detective produces a 9mm pistol found in the bush close to the Guest House. Forensic checks show it to be covered only in

Lucas's fingerprints. It has been fired recently. Pule is waiting for the ballistics report on the bullet taken out of April Coetzee's head and he expects it will confirm that the weapon in the sealed plastic bag on the table in front of Lucas is the one that killed her.

Lucas, feeling like the support actor in a movie, agrees that the pistol is his. Two parallel strands of thought are processing; he thinks of the licence that he holds and the matter of minutes needed for the detective to confirm its ownership. Indeed, he has already done this. At the same time, he is tracing the whereabouts of his gun during the previous evening and trying to pinpoint where he let it fall into the hands of the Mozambicans.

The detective suggests Lucas calls his attorney.

While waiting for his attorney to arrive, Lucas again retreats into his memories of childhood. His father had been typical of his generation; only just literate with few aspirations. His job as a gardener was about the best he could hope for. He was not political; he was mostly accepting of his place in the racist society that was all he had ever known. Most of the whites he encountered were benevolent and as he rarely (never, in Lucas's experience) stepped across the boundaries set for the black man in Apartheid society he did not provoke their potential anger. He liked to spend times with his son telling stories of the old days when he came to the Lowveld to work on the newly planted citrus plantations.

When he was about twelve, Lucas joined his father on a trip to Johannesburg to meet his grandmother for the first time. It was the furthest he had ever travelled and promised to be quite an adventure. Father and son set off early one Saturday morning on foot hoping to get a lift on the west going N4. They were soon picked up by an Indian man in his VW Kombi. The man was going all the way to Johannesburg to pick up his shop goods for the following month. He was happy to take them along. His black assistant was travelling in the front seat and Lucas settled first into the seat behind him and next to his father. Later he was invited to climb into the front and sit in the middle of the bench seat. The three men and young Lucas chatted easily in a mixture of English, Zulu and Afrikaans. The driver shared his padkos with them. Lucas ate samosas and butter chicken wrapped in roti bread. He could still bring the flavours to mind after all the intervening years.

At one point in the trip, around midday, and miles from anywhere, the Kombi stopped to allow the Indian man to get out, taking a small colourful carpet and a bottle of water with him. He walked a few yards away from the road into the veld. The man looked at the sun then the road and seemed to orient himself before placing his carpet on the ground. Then he washed his hands, mouth, nose, arms, face, head, ears and finally his feet, sparingly using the water from the bottle. Lucas's father explained that the man was about to pray. The prayer took just a few minutes before the man returned to the Kombi and its passengers.

The journey took seven hours and Lucas and his father were dropped in Fordsburg from where they took a bus to Kliptown where his grandmother was living. They agreed to meet the Indian man, on Monday morning for the journey back home. The trip represented a kind of rite of passage in Lucas's mind. He had been in the company of men and treated like a man for the first time.

Lucas reflects on the old days and is surprised that he feels a sense of nostalgia. Then ordinary people were somehow more open and friendlier, less frightened and less preoccupied with money. Apartheid was evil but it did not define the souls of ordinary folk. People helped each other because life was difficult for everyone unless you were wealthy. These days, an Indian man driving to Joburg would probably be too frightened to pick up a black man and his son; imagining a gang of accomplices emerging from the bush intent on hijack or robbery. The insecurity is for the most part misplaced but it only needs the occasional horror story to keep people on their guard. Everybody has their own horror story even if is usually third hand by the time it is retold.

The trip to his grandmother was memorable. The old lady spoiled him for the short time he was with her and she sent him back with ten rand in his pocket. He had only met her once. She died when he was fourteen and his father had travelled alone to her funeral. Taking the whole family would have been unaffordable.

*

The attorney arrives and Lucas is forced out of his reverie before it reaches the Kombi ride back to the Lowveld. The attorney has heard, on his arrival at the police station, that the bullet that caused April's fatal wound was fired by Lucas's gun. Lucas covers the details of the evening of the murder and emphasises his innocence. The attorney warns Lucas that he is going to be charged and there is no chance of bail.

Chapter 11
Sunday Lunch

Doctor is reading the Sunday Times. His article has been published covering the murder of April and the results of his investigation into apparently corrupt payments in which she was involved along with Lucas. The headline reads "Mpumalanga Murder Opens Can of Worms".

Around mid-morning, his cell phone rings and it is Detective Pule. He has also been reading the article and is annoyed that Doctor had not shared his investigation with him earlier. The story provides a clear motive for Lucas as the prime suspect. He suspects that Doctor is holding back on some of the details of the story. What is he going to be writing next week? Doctor feels no remorse. He had answered the detective's questions honestly and completely. Maybe he had not asked the right questions. The detective ends the call; he is not happy.

The next call is from Hlengiwe, back from Church, who has just read his article and is full of praise. She suggests they meet for lunch. He does not need persuading and he agrees to pick her up at her Mother's house in an hour.

Just a few minutes later, Doctor receives a call from a producer at 702 Radio. She wants him to go on live in just a few minutes time to answer questions about the murder and his investigation. He agrees. It is the first time he has been on radio. He collects his thoughts just in time for the call back from the producer who puts him through live to the studio. The programme host asks him to recap his story and then probes him about the line of his further investigation. He is reluctant to say much but tries to build up a sense of suspense around the idea that there is more scandal to be exposed.

Towards the end of the interview, the interviewer asks him about himself suggesting the audience are keen to hear how a poor Sowetan has made a success out of journalism. He finds himself opening up about his recovery from alcoholism and putting his life back on track. Listening to himself he is surprised to find himself being quite so open. This part of his life is not something he is proud of and he is normally much more reticent.

Doctor arrives at Hlengiwe's a little more than an hour after her call. He explains the radio interview. She is pleased to see him and excited about the interview even though she missed it. Hlengiwe's mother appears and greets him warmly. She had been in the congregation on the previous Sunday and has no trouble connecting him to his father whom she remembers from her school days. Hlengiwe and Doctor make their excuses and head out to a restaurant near White River. On the way, they catch an extract from his interview that is playing on the hourly 702 news bulletin. They also stop at the mall and she chooses a shirt for him. He leaves the store wearing it. Now he is at least part way to looking the part as Hlengiwe's boyfriend. She is wearing a light summer dress which accentuates her tall, slim figure. Doctor is smitten again.

The afternoon is warm and the couple take their time over lunch on a terrace that looks out over citrus farms and towards the mountains between Mbombela and Barberton. The food is good and the restaurant not the kind of place that Doctor would normally feel comfortable. Hlengiwe, though, seems at home;

71

probably she is used to business lunches in such places. They talk lightly about their childhoods, their schooling and the problems of their country. They hold hands across the table and the connection they feel, but do not speak of, is tangible to both of them.

Thunder clouds are building in the direction of the mountains and there is the promise of a storm to break the winter drought. Doctor hopes it will not be a false promise. He is looking forward to the summer.

Doctor pays the bill and is grateful for the fee that will soon be in his bank account.

The new couple take a drive north towards Sabie. They find a quiet spot, spread a blanket and watch the late afternoon shadows creep out from the escarpment. The storm clouds have become dramatic towers framing the sinking sun. The rain will probably fall elsewhere. For the moment, they have no need of further conversation. Doctor is intoxicated by the smell of the veld and Hlengiwe's perfume.

Chapter 12
Pardon

On Monday morning, Doctor heads again to the guest house and finds Mrs Raworth sitting at her desk in the office behind the Reception area. She is not sure how to feel about his arrival and grudgingly offers him a seat opposite her. He notices that her hands are trembling. Clearly, she was not expecting her dubious dealings to end in a murder. She mentions that the police have been asking questions about her business relationship with Promovest. He notices that she has a copy of the Sunday Times on her desk and he guesses that she has been smart enough to confirm the relatively minor flows of money that Doctor's investigations have already exposed. She is expecting that she will be charged although the police have suggested that maybe she can turn witness in return for the charges being dropped. Only now has she realized that the deal she has done with April and Lucas has made her very little money. Probably she was just trying to keep her occupancy high.

Doctor asks about the CCTV recordings from the night of the murder. Mrs Raworth mentions that the police seized them and her laptop during a visit first thing this morning. Doctor is surprised that they had not done that earlier and wonders if she had checked the recordings herself. She opens up unexpectedly and mentions a Land Cruiser that arrived around one thirty a.m. and two men going into April's chalet. Three men left at two fifteen a.m. The Land Cruiser returned an hour later and just one man entered her chalet for a very short period before re-joining the Land Cruiser which left in a hurry. With unexpected foresight, she had put a copy of the CCTV footage on a flash drive that she plugs into another laptop before showing Doctor the sequence she has described. The Land Cruiser must be the Mozambicans but the night footage is not clear enough to read the plates. The vehicle was parked some way from the building during the second visit of the night, just failing to elude the camera. Maybe the police will be able to enhance the images and get a lead. At any rate, they must now have some doubts about the role played by Lucas.

Doctor is about to ask Raworth whether there is anything else he should know about her dealings with April and Lucas; she seems to be willing to talk. His phone rings. It is Pardon Nozulu. She got his number from Joy Mpofu. She sounds frightened. She needs to see him urgently. They agree to meet at her home before lunch.

The moment has gone and Mrs Raworth is no longer in the mood for sharing information. He decides not to push her and leaves.

On the road to the Nozulu home near Hazyview, Doctor again takes stock of his investigation. It is clear now that the Promovest payments are not the main story. The Mozambicans, the murder that they probably committed and the large payments made to their company in which Lucas's wife has a share are adding up to something pretty big even by South Africa's sad standards of corruption. He wonders if April was aware of this bigger game. Probably not he thinks. He wonders how far behind him the police are in working it out. What else is there to discover?

The Nozulu home is on a country estate of fifty or so ostentatious homes on large stands. A group of Impala stare, motionless, at him as he drives through the security barrier at the entrance. Pardon is waiting for him on the driveway leading to her front

74

door. The Nozulu's have been investing their wealth in a lifestyle they could only have dreamt of as children.

While waiting she thinks back to her first date with Lucas. They had both just finished their matric. exams and were looking forward to the Christmas holidays. They took a kombi taxi into Mbombela, Nelspruit as it was in those days, where they watched a film and then had milk shakes. At the time it seemed very sophisticated and Lucas impressed her with his confidence and ambition. He was her only boyfriend and they had been a team ever since or so she thought.

Pardon greets Doctor cautiously, leads him into the house and offers him tea which her maid is sent off to fix. He takes a seat on the edge of a rich, dark brown leather sofa in the double height lounge surrounded by a gallery that he presumes gives entry to the bedrooms. A couple of ceiling fans turn unnecessarily; the room is cool. Pardon seems to have recovered her composure since the phone call. Doctor asks her about Lucas. He is still being held but has been charged so far only with fraud. He will appear before a magistrate later today. His lawyer is confident that he will get bail. Doctor thinks this must mean that the police have taken a close look at the CCTV and concluded that Lucas is probably not the murderer.

Pardon is worried. The local police have handed over the further investigation of the fraud case to the Hawks, though they are continuing to lead the hunt for April's murderers. Her bank accounts have been frozen. Doctor is not sure why she thinks he can help her. Pardon explains that Lucas has asked her to speak to him and to give him the address in Maputo where he might find the Mozambicans. He is worried that since they are no longer in

South Africa, the Hawks may choose to hang the whole story around his neck. She hands him a letter from a Mozambican company, XaiXai Investments. The company directors mentioned in small print on the footer of the letter are the same Mozambicans involved in the successful irrigation bid.

The maid reappears with the tea and Pardon stops talking. Doctor thanks her, promises to think about how he can use the information and leaves his tea undrunk. He already knows what he will do next.

As he is passing through the security gate, a convoy of three white Golfs, blue lights flashing, with the familiar red and yellow hawk logo emblazoned on the vehicles' sides, is waiting to be let in. Pardon is going to have a busy morning. He discreetly takes a photograph of the convoy as it passes through the entry barrier.

Doctor stops to call his editor and updates him on the latest developments. The editor undertakes to post the breaking news of the Hawks involvement and their morning raid in Hazyview. Another small fee has been earned. It will be a while before anyone else gets the story. Doctor WhatsApp's the photograph and shares his plan to travel to Maputo. Promising to be careful, he will have another chapter in the story for the coming Sunday's paper. The best way for him to help Lucas is to ensure the Mozambicans' story is exposed. He is not sure why he feels sorry for Lucas and Pardon. Lucas is corrupt and people he grew up with are poorer because of him. That is hard to forgive but Doctor is grateful to Lucas for his earlier rescue and keen to see justice for the murdered April even if she was also a fraud.

Doctor next calls Hlengiwe. She is on her way to a site in Malelane but she offers to join him on the trip to Maputo. She is sure she can clear a few days leave with her boss. Doctor is not sure she should accompany him but the prospect of some time together is too much to resist. They both realize at this point that neither of them has a passport. They agree to meet at Home Affairs in Mbombela and try to fast track their applications.

The Home Affairs office, in Voortrekker Street, is a rough and ready place with rows of plastic chairs for the queuing people who are applying for new identity cards, work permits and passports. Nobody is in a good mood. The customers are losing pay while they sit here grumbling and unsure if they are in the right queue; the older ones remembering the days when they came here for their Book of Life or passes to travel inside their own country. Those behind the counters have forgotten their customer service training. The obscure mission statement proudly displayed above the counter grills does not suggest customers are likely to be a priority. Most of the people arriving at the counter are quickly sent away with more forms to fill in and doomed to spend more time in the queue. Hlengiwe spots someone she knows with a staff pass around her neck and heading upstairs to offices out of bounds to the public. She calls to her and explains the reason for their visit. Hlengiwe's friend, despite being obviously distracted by her good-looking companion, gets the right forms and sends them through to have their passport photographs taken and fingerprints verified. The forms are mercifully straightforward because they have current identity cards and for a small extra fee the passports will be ready on Wednesday morning. Doctor reflects that at least this office appears to be a haven from the storm of corruption and remembers the time when his mother had had to buy an electric kettle for the woman behind the counter in order to get a copy of his full birth certificate. Her application would have otherwise been put to the bottom of a pile of others that were destined to be lost or processed much later in an annual clear up of the backlog.

Hlengiwe insists that Doctor travels with her to Malelane for her delayed site visit so they can make the most of the rest of the day. He relaxes in the passenger seat of her Golf and thinks ahead to Maputo and how he will handle the next phase of his investigation while avoiding a confrontation with the Mozambicans who will probably be out for his blood. Hlengiwe meets the architect who has waited for her since the morning and agrees some changes that the client has requested. She will need to work out some revised costings but that can wait until tomorrow. They head back to KaBokweni and supper with Lukhele family.

Chapter 13
Maputo

The passports are ready for collection on Wednesday morning as promised. Doctor is again being driven by Hlengiwe. He would have happily taken his Polo but she had thought the Golf would be more comfortable. She is right. It is a glorious spring day and promises to be hot by the time they reach the Indian Ocean at Maputo. The Crocodile River is running lazily through its narrow ravine before Malelane where it widens out and forms the southern limit of the Kruger National Park. When the rains come it will become a torrent.

Over the last couple of days, Doctor has been trying to find out more about XaiXai Investments. The company owns several businesses in Mozambique and the Irrigation Company in South Africa. The businesses include an office cleaning company in Maputo and a farm on the coast north of the capital near the town of XaiXai. The most recent investment appears to be the acquisition of an Oil and Gas Services company; XaiXai Investments is growing fast. There seems to be no lack of funds.

They reach the Lebombo border post at eleven in the morning. The queue on the South African side is dominated by large ore carrying tipper trucks taking their loads to the sea and the hungry Chinese bulk carriers awaiting them.

Hlengiwe parks her car and the couple walk over to the customs building ignoring the haranguing agents soliciting for business. The forms that need to be filled in to allow the car to cross the border are tedious but straightforward. With their stamped customs clearance they walk through to the passport inspection area where there is a short queue. They return to the car, drive through the border and stop to have a further inspection of their papers by the Mozambican border police who are noticeably less surly than their counterparts. Then they are on their way towards the Ocean.

After the short drop down from the Lebombo ridge, the seventy-minute drive to Maputo is mostly through flat, arid land that had been, three decades earlier, one big minefield as the warring parties in the civil war struggled to finish each other off.

During the drive, Hlengiwe gently asks him about his alcoholism. Doctor is initially hesitant. He tries to order his thoughts and launches tentatively into the story.

Doctor was working as a porter in a Sandton hotel, writing in his spare time and only occasionally getting his work published. His girlfriend, with whom he had been living for about a year, had lost her job in the cosmetics section of a department store. She became depressed and dysfunctional. They had both used drugs occasionally when they went clubbing but now her use escalated rapidly into dependency. She was caught shoplifting. Doctor's wages evaporated before the middle of the month; mostly spent on her drugs and their alcohol. Doctor started to drink heavily in an attempt to stay tuned in to his girlfriend. For some reason the drugs did not seduce him. Then his girlfriend left. He heard she had moved in with a drug dealer who had money to feed her habit. Later he heard that the drug dealer had been arrested for her murder. Pretty much the only thing she left behind was her depression which now dragged Doctor into some very dark depths. Doctor was evicted from his small flat and took to sleeping rough under an elevated section of highway between

Sandton and Marlboro. He quickly lost his own job as his boss at the hotel acted to prevent his body odour from offending the paying clients.

It was at this point that his fortunes changed and the old varsity friend came to his rescue. The friend had been out of touch for some time. He called Doctor out of the blue expecting to arrange a civilised drink one evening and catch up. Somehow, Doctor had kept his phone and even though he had no air time, he could receive his friend's call. The friend could barely hear Doctor above the sound of Johannesburg traffic thundering above his head. Doctor sounded terrible; nothing like the garrulous companion of their study days. Doctor told him where he was and a few minutes later, the friend arrived to take him home. From here the difficult road to recovery rolled out into Doctor's future.

*

As they enter the Maputo suburbs, they are forced to stop at a police roadblock. The officer is polite and apparently taken with the beautiful Swazi driver to whom he offers a lecherous grin. He inspects the customs clearance and Hlengiwe's driver's license. There is a problem. He waves the car into the verge and leaves them while he talks to his colleague who has just completed a search of a local car which is now pulling away. The colleague approaches Hlengiwe's car. Doctor has decided that a fifty-rand note might be the solution to the problem and he reaches across Hlengiwe to offer his passport with the note enclosed. The officer casually takes the note, hands the passport back and gestures for them to move on.

81

Delagoa Bay, and the Indian Ocean beyond, is as blue as the pictures in the travel brochures. There are several Arab Dhow fishing boats at anchor close to the shore; their off-white lateen sails furled on deck. Doctor and Hlengiwe find a comfortable guest house near the beach front and settle into their room. It is the first time they have had complete privacy and they are in a hurry to take advantage of it.

Later they take a walk, arm in arm, along the beach front. They settle on the terrace of a little restaurant and order LM prawns, a succulent reminder of the city's colonial name; Lourenço Marques. The view from the restaurant takes in the harbour where a fleet of rusting tuna boats are testament to more corruption and mismanagement. Doctor recalls that they are the reason behind the economic crisis from which Mozambique has yet to recover. The son of the president is under arrest awaiting trial for his part in the two-billion-dollar debt scandal.

Sunset is still before six but the breeze off the sea is warm. Hlengiwe wears a colourful shawl over her shoulders but her long legs are bare. Doctor notices the glow on her face and feels himself falling more deeply in love with her. She in turn runs her hand over his head in her trademark sign of affection.

The next morning after an early breakfast, the two would-be tourists locate the office of XaiXai Investments. It is in a colonial style, white-washed bungalow that has a view over the city and its blue bay. They park a little way up the street and settle down to watch the comings and goings. Their surveillance is just a few minutes old when the Land Cruiser that Doctor had seen in Hazyview drives up and parks outside the office. He recognises the driver, who is alone, as the one of the men that met with Lucas on that Saturday. He is a middle-aged Portuguese and Doctor reckons that he is not particularly fit. If he needs to fight him or run he judges he can cope. Hopefully, though, he is not armed.

Forgetting his earlier resolution to avoid a premature confrontation, and leaving Hlengiwe in the Golf, Doctor walks down to the office and rings the bell. A woman answers and he introduces himself as Doctor Lukhele, a journalist from Johannesburg. He is hoping to see Luis Da Costa or Francisco Pereira. The door release buzzes. The woman is at a reception desk. Several doors lead beyond the reception area. One is a toilet and name plates on two of the doors match the names of the men he is seeking. The receptionist knocks on the door of Luis Da Costa and announces Doctor who takes a business card from the reception desk and moves towards the office.

Inside, Doctor's proffered handshake is not accepted. Instead he is motioned to a seat opposite Da Costa who is slouched in his chair and tapping away on his laptop keyboard. A black coffee is cooling next to the laptop and the woman asks Doctor if he would also take one. He thanks her and accepts.

Da Costa says nothing. Doctor waits for a few seconds and then explains that he is researching government procurement practices in South Africa and that he has been working on a story involving the tenders for an irrigation project in Mpumalanga which he knows was won by XaiXai's South African subsidiary. He asks Da Costa what his experience has been of the provincial government's tender and award process. Da Costa shrugs and suggests that it was rather efficient. Doctor asks about his South African company's lack of a Black Empowerment rating and Da Costa shrugs again indicating that that is being fixed; the company is newly established and these things take time. Doctor casually drops in a comment about Pardon's role as a Company Director and asks if that is part of the fix. Da Costa sits up and looks more interested in the conversation. He goes to his phone and texts a message while describing the training programme that he is setting up for the new employees.

Doctor goes for the jugular and asks about the large pre-payment the company has received. Now Da Costa looks rattled. He mentions the significant start-up costs that he is incurring but expresses his growing impatience and that perhaps Doctor should look elsewhere for a story.

The receptionist returns with Doctor's coffee but Da Costa waves her away and announces that Doctor is leaving.

Back on the street, Doctor looks up the road to where he left Hlengiwe. The Golf is gone. He looks around, hoping that Hlengiwe has moved to a new position, but he immediately knows he will not find her or the car. He connects Da Costa's text. She and her car have disappeared.

A large hole opens up in the pit of his stomach. He had ignored his intuition and brought Hlengiwe along. Now it is going horribly wrong. He jogs downhill back to the guest house hoping against hope that she had decided to return.

There is no Golf or Hlengiwe at the guest house.

Chapter 14
Court Appearance

Lucas is handcuffed in an unmarked car which is making the two hundred metre journey to the Magistrate Court. The journey is no more than a two-minute walk but the police are taking no chances. The car pulls up at the rear of the courthouse, where there are a small number of journalists and cameramen gathered. Lucas is helped out of the back and led into the building before there is any possibility of him responding to the barrage of shouted questions. Another cell awaits him. The policeman escorting him motions him in and offers his parting suggestion that he may be waiting sometime.

Lucas's mind returns to his childhood and the watershed trip to visit his grandmother. The trip back to his home in the Lowveld had started badly. The taxi, that they took from Kliptown downtown to Noord Street, suffered a puncture and while the driver was fitting the spare, a couple of police officers arrived and started to check the passes of the passengers. Lucas's father handed his passbook to one of the officers, a slight, white man of no more than twenty. The officer examined the pass carefully and found the entry allowing travel to Johannesburg which was valid for another week. He looked at Lucas and asked him for his pass. He was frightened and unable to say anything. His father confirmed that Lucas was only twelve and did not have a pass. The policeman grunted. He took his pen from his uniform jacket and crossed out the vital entry in his father's book. At a careless stroke they were illegal. The policeman told his father to get back home today. His father agreed, referring to the officer as master. Lucas had not encountered this kind of treatment before and he was ashamed that his father had to humble himself in this manner.

Lucas and his father faced a forty-minute walk across town from the taxi rank to Fordsburg where they were hoping to meet the Indian man who had promised to take them home. They arrived over an hour after the agreed time. To their surprise, the Kombi was still waiting for them. They climbed in and were soon headed towards the Eastern Transvaal; relieved to be leaving Johannesburg and its hostile authorities but sad in the knowledge that they might not see Gogo Nozulu again.

*

The cell door opens and Lucas's attorney enters. They shake hands and the attorney briefs Lucas on the expected course of the hearing in front of the magistrate. The hearing should be very short. The police will oppose bail because they are reluctant to release a suspect in April's murder even though they now have evidence that he is not the murderer. For the moment he is to be charged with fraud and misconduct related to corruption activities.

Lucas is led into the courtroom. The magistrate enters and Lucas recognises her immediately as someone he was at school with. There is no suggestion of recognition from her however.

The prosecutor outlines the case against Lucas and recommends the case is referred to the High Court for hearing before a judge. In the meantime, Lucas should be remanded in custody.

The attorney appearing for Lucas requests bail, explaining that there is no risk of him fleeing the country and that he poses no risk to the community.

To Lucas's surprise, the magistrate agrees to bail and asks her legal advisor to have the case listed for the High Court at the earliest opportunity.

Lucas is led out of the courtroom and Pardon is waiting to greet him. She hugs him hard. She will be angry later. Lucas is handed a plastic bag containing the personal items he had handed over at the time of his arrest. His phone has been held by the police,

Chapter 15
The Farm

Hlengiwe awakes to find herself in unfamiliar surroundings. She starts to piece together the last few hours. She remembers a man getting into the passenger seat of her car. She had not noticed anyone approaching. It was not Doctor. The man looked like a Portuguese. She remembered he had a neat beard but little else. He said nothing, leant across and put a cloth over her mouth and nose. There was an overpowering medicinal smell and then she passed out.

She is in a dark room and one wrist is handcuffed to a bed. There is a sliver of sunlight coming through a gap in the curtains and as her eyes become accustomed to the low level of light she takes in that the room is almost bare and the walls roughly plastered. There is an animal smell; possibly horses. She can hear doves outside. Then she hears African voices speaking Portuguese.

Hlengiwe feels surprisingly calm. She is angry with herself for being such an easy target. She had not locked her car doors while waiting for Doctor and she had not been alert to the possibility of someone creeping up to the car. She wishes she could tell Doctor that she is OK.

The door of the room opens and a woman enters with a plate of food and a glass of water. Hlengiwe asks her where she is but the woman answers in Portuguese which she cannot understand. She thinks she hears the name XaiXai. She knows that is a place north of Maputo and she knows from Doctor that XaiXai Investments have a farm there. She guesses that she is probably at the farm.

Chapter 16
The Raid

Doctor finds a police station and tries to make himself understood to the policeman behind the counter. The policeman speaks no English and, after a few minutes of frustrating shrugs and apparent glimpses of comprehension, he gestures Doctor towards a line of upright chairs against the wall of the room. After a thirty-minute wait, a tall, plain clothes man arrives and introduces himself as André Du Toit. His name and his strong Afrikaner accent suggest he is a South African. His deep suntan suggests that maybe several generations ago his Dutch blood had been mixed with African but, of course, he would be horrified by any such suggestion.

Doctor retells the story of the morning, giving the minimum amount of background detail. Du Toit listens carefully and then makes a call, speaking Portuguese now as if it is his first language.

André Du Toit is a South African police liaison officer, based in Maputo, who spends his days investigating gangs involved in human trafficking and drug smuggling across the border and toward the bright lights and money of Johannesburg. In the course of his work, he has come across Luis Da Costa and his associates but he has never been able to build a convincing case against them or XaiXai Investments. He does know the farm and he is confident that if Hlengiwe has been kidnapped she will be there. Meantime, he needs to find out what else Doctor knows.

André fixes a stare on Doctor and asks him to explain what exactly it is that he is investigating. Doctor is reluctant to share his story but he is too worried about Hlengiwe to hold back. It takes him nearly an hour to bring Du Toit up to speed.

Darkness comes quickly just after five thirty. Five Mozambican policemen led by a sergeant are already staked out close to the farmhouse. They are lightly armed with nine-millimetre pistols. The sergeant is a veteran of the long civil war and is used to being in this kind of situation. His men are much younger and less experienced. He can tell they are nervous and excited in equal measure. The farmhouse is lit up but the outhouses are only visible in outline. A woman leaves the house and heads for one of the outhouses. A small window suggests the inside is dimly lit. She seems to be carrying food. A floodlight responds to her movement and bathes the outhouses in a stark white light. She pushes open the door with her foot and goes inside. From the farmhouse comes the sound of laughter. A group of men are settling in for the evening. The sergeant listens to their chatter and estimates there are maybe three or four of them.

The woman returns to the house and the outhouses are once again barely visible.

The sergeant motions to his men and they move swiftly and silently toward the same door that the woman had just exited. The sergeant has been worrying that the door he had expected to be locked is obviously not so. He reasons that there must be another door inside that is secured and beyond which they will find the kidnapped woman they are tasked to rescue.

The sergeant and one of his men are at each side of the door while the other three take positions around the two sides of the outhouse. Their earlier reconnaissance established that the rear has no windows or doors. With their pistols cocked and ready, the two men burst in through the door. Inside three children sit around a small table eating pizza. One of them screams at the sight of the armed policemen. The sergeant, realises it can only be seconds before the men in the farmhouse, alerted by the scream, reach them. He scans the room and notices two other doors. He motions to his partner to check one of them while he takes the other. They are both unlocked and there is no sign of Hlengiwe in either of them. Then they are on the way out, running.

The other three policemen have seen the men come out of the farmhouse. The sergeant shouts to them to get back to the truck that they had parked about five hundred metres away in the bush but close to the road. He is reluctant to get into a fight when it seems they may have been on a fool's errand.

The recently carousing men, with the woman close behind them, make it to the outhouse. The woman and one of the men go inside and the other men, four of them, wait for a few seconds then respond to shouted instructions from inside to spread out and look for the intruders. They are armed with AK-47s.

The sergeant and his platoon reach their truck and pile into the open back. They had left the driver and now he has the engine running and the truck pointed in the direction of the road. A few seconds later they re-join the road. Somehow, two of the armed men from the farmhouse are on the road in front of them. They spray the truck with bullets; aiming mainly for the tyres but a stray bullet smashes through the windscreen and the driver slumps over the wheel. The truck veers off the road and overturns. The sergeant and two of his men are thrown clear of the truck as it comes to a rest. They are dazed but able to find cover and draw their pistols as the AK-47s close cautiously on the truck. The sergeant is able to pick off one of the men but is killed instantly by the rapid fire that comes in reply. The two surviving policemen, without their experienced sergeant, stand with their arms raised in surrender.

Back in Maputo, André Du Toit receives a call from XaiXai. The rescue mission has not returned and there has been no message from the platoon since the driver called in to relay a message from his sergeant to say that they were in position close to the farmhouse. Now it is approaching midnight and another platoon had been sent to investigate.

André passes on the news to Doctor who has refused to leave the police station. Doctor is by now distraught.

Not very far away, Da Costa is calling Junior Khumalo.

Chapter 17
The Hawks

Lucas is feeling a little better after a night in his own bed. He and Pardon share a silent breakfast on the stoep of their home while their gardener weeds the paving around the pool. The weaver birds are noisily renovating their nests in a thorn tree just beyond the garden.

The gardener moves further away from the stoep and Pardon can contain her anger no longer. She demands to know just exactly what is going on. Lucas is at first evasive; at least partly because he is trying to get the complicated story straight in his own mind. He realises he is going to need Pardon's full support if he is to emerge with anything at all from the mess he has created so he decides to tell her everything. He is vague about his relationship with April but Pardon is not willing to let him get away with that and he is forced to admit his infidelity too. Pardon is incandescent and pummels him ineffectually before breaking down in uncontrollable sobs.

While Lucas is trying and failing to calm his wife, her mobile rings. Lucas takes the call. It is a security guard at the gate of the estate. The Hawks are here again.

This time there is just one car but its markings ensure that Lucas is further embarrassed in the eyes of his neighbours. Captain Thabo Mkhize comes to the front door alone. His driver waits in the car. Lucas greets Mkhize sullenly and invites him into the lounge. Pardon has hurried, tearfully, upstairs to their bedroom. He watches as Mkhize scans the room and takes in the evidence of wealth accumulation. The lifestyle that Lucas and Pardon have adopted would require something more lucrative than the fiddling of expenses and skimming the proceeds of one or two dubious contracts. Actually, until quite recently, Lucas had been living beyond his means and his home is still heavily mortgaged. He realises this had made him more susceptible to the temptations offered by the Mozambicans only just over a year ago. Until recently, the cars he and Pardon drove were quite unremarkable but he had enjoyed the experience of buying new with cash and surprising Pardon. If only he had been less greedy.

Mkhize has seen it before. He should be contemptuous but he needs to try to develop a rapport with Lucas to give him the best chance of getting to the full extent of the corruption.

Mkhize begins formally and reminds Lucas that he can choose to have his attorney present but suggests that maybe a more relaxed conversation can be helpful to both of them. Lucas agrees. The Hawk explains that he is responsible for investigating financial irregularities that he thinks Lucas has been involved in. April's murder is not part of his investigation although he is aware that his police colleagues now believe he did not fire the gun that killed her. Nevertheless, he is implicated. He needs to know more about the men that he was with on the night of her murder. If Lucas can help him then maybe he can recommend leniency. So far Lucas has not admitted knowledge of his Mozambican colleagues but he realises he is going to have to explain that relationship if he is to avoid being charged with involvement in the murder. He knows already that he will likely be convicted for his role in April's expenses fraud and the payments to Promovest from which he received a regular kickback. How can he limit the damage beyond that? The Mozambicans probably expect him to betray them so there is not much to be lost now in revealing their role in his story. They are unlikely to be travelling into South Africa in the near future anyway and it seems the police are already onto them otherwise he would certainly have been charged with April's murder already. Perhaps to his credit, Lucas has never developed a skill for lying. He decides the best course is to lay out his story. Lucas's descent into corruption started some ten years ago so it is going to take a while.

Two hours later, Lucas is finished. Mkhize interrupted a few times with questions but mostly it was Lucas in full flow. Mkhize asks Lucas if he is prepared to make a statement to confirm what he has told him. Lucas hesitates and promises to discuss this with his attorney.

Mkhize is interested to find out if there are other, perhaps more senior figures involved but he decides to leave this for the moment and until he has had a chance to do some investigation himself. So far, this case has been too easy. Most of the hard work is the result of Doctor Lukhele's efforts for the Sunday Times. The experienced Hawk has a hunch that there is still more to discover.

Mkhize gets up as if to leave but not before he drops a bomb on Lucas. Tomorrow morning, he has arranged for a truck to pick up most of the furniture and appliances in the Nozulu home and the couple's two cars. Lucas is stunned and protests feebly but Mkhize is already headed for the door and his waiting driver. He feels good that his powers allow him to make life uncomfortable for Lucas and his wife. Hopefully, this is just the beginning.

Back in the car, Mkhize makes a call to his deputy. A dawn raid by a team of forensic auditors has been underway for some hours now and he wants an update. They are camped out in the offices of the Provincial Administration and right now Joy Mpofu is helping a member of the team to navigate the index of archived documents. Everyone in the building is stunned and several are frightened.

Chapter 18
Relapse

Doctor is in a bar on the seafront. He has been there for several hours and after the initial high of his first drink in over a year, he is now in a deep depression. He feels helpless. The news of the fateful raid on the farmhouse seems to have undone the months of careful reconstruction of his soul. Unable to face returning to the guest house that he had shared with Hlengiwe, he could only think of this self-destruction as a way of coping. But it is not working and unlike the dedicated alcoholic he once was, he is able to recognise that it is not working. He orders a black coffee and starts to think about his next move. He cannot be sure Hlengiwe is still alive but the prospect of living without her is now so bleak that he has to believe she is still being held somewhere. Where would she be if not in the XaiXai farmhouse? She could be anywhere of course and given the ruthless murder of April there is little chance they will spare his lover unless they can see value in holding her.

André has told him to stay in Maputo and assured him the police are doing all they can to find Hlengiwe. But it is not in the sober Doctor's nature to do nothing.

Nursing a horrible hangover and without too much thought, Doctor retrieves the business card from his pocket and calls Luis Da Costa's mobile.

Da Costa picks up. The South African number is not one of his contacts but he is not surprised to hear a miserable sounding, but unmistakeable Doctor on the call. Without introducing himself, Doctor offers himself as a hostage in exchange for Hlengiwe. Da

Costa feigns surprise and says he has no idea who Hlengiwe is or what he is talking about. Besides, his business was doing just fine until he poked his nose in and now he is facing awkward questions from all sides. Why should he entertain Doctor?

Doctor mentions his next, as yet unwritten, article for the Sunday Times and suggests that maybe he could hold off sending it in return for Hlengiwe's safety.

Da Costa suggests they meet later that evening at the Polana Hotel.

Chapter 19
Escape

Hlengiwe is breathless from running and is hidden in the bush by the track. She is very scared. She can hear voices close by and see torchlight probing the darkness. It is ten minutes since she managed to escape from her Golf in which she was being moved. They had been driving for maybe half an hour when the car stopped at a junction. She surprised herself, the driver and the guard sitting next to her in the back seat, by opening the door and running. Her hands were tied together in front of her but she was able to make it to a narrow track that disappeared into the bush before her captors were able to set off in pursuit. She ran faster than she thought possible, narrowly avoiding falling several times, handicapped by her bound hands. Now she could only hope that her hiding place would not be discovered. While recovering her breath she tried to piece together the last hour or so.

She had been sleeping fitfully in the dark loft space of what she had decided was a barn. There were children's voices coming from the room below. Then the children's chatter had turned to screams. She could not be sure but she guessed that some kind of rescue mission had come close to finding her. Over the next few minutes there was shouting, vehicles starting up and then gunfire not far away.

Then silence.

After what was probably only fifteen minutes but seemed much longer, the trap door to the loft opened and a shaft of light entered from the room below. A man came up through the trap door and grabbed her roughly by one arm bringing her unsteadily to a standing position. Then she was bundled through the trap door and half caught, half man-handled to the floor. The abandoned pizzas were still on the table but the children had disappeared. The next thing she knew, she was in the back of her own car and driving away from the farmhouse and past a wrecked police truck, headlights on and lying at a precarious angle in the ditch at the side of the track. The windscreen of the truck was shattered. She started to formulate a plan of escape and waited for her opportunity which came when the car made a stop at the junction near where she now lay hidden.

The voices and the torchlight were closing in on her position when she heard another vehicle skid to a halt in the direction she had come. She thought she could see a flashing blue light through the thick bush. Then she heard more voices. The torchlight disappeared to be replaced by a stronger flashlight. She decided to run towards it. She broke cover and ran. Then someone in front of her shouted to her to stop. She froze, half expecting to be shot. A uniformed figure emerged from the blinding light and called her Hlengiwe. She burst into tears. He hugged her briefly before cutting the plastic cords binding her wrists. The policeman spoke very little English but enough to reassure her she was safe. One of his team would drive her car back to XaiXai and she was eased gently into the passenger seat for the short journey. The South African plates on her car had probably saved her; the police might otherwise have passed the scene of her escape.

The police team make a quick, unsuccessful search of the area, looking for Hlengiwe's kidnappers. They have melted into the bush and anyway the officer that had met Hlengiwe is anxious to confirm the fate of his colleagues. They drive fast towards the farmhouse. The first platoon's half capsized truck is easily spotted.

The dead driver is slumped over the wheel and two officers are dead, necks broken, in the back. The body of the sergeant is nearby. Two men are missing. The farmhouse is deserted.

Chapter 20
Polana

At about the same time as Hlengiwe's escape, Doctor arrives at the Polana Hotel. The colonial style, white building was the place to stay when the Portuguese were enjoying the charms of their capital, Lourenço Marques. Four decades and a long civil war later, it is still Maputo's finest hotel. Overlooking the Indian Ocean, the cool interiors are furnished in early twentieth century style. Doctor feels decidedly out of place. He heads for the lounge bar and finds Da Costa in a discreet corner.

Doctor had expected to be met by Da Costa and probably one or two of his tough guys. In fact, he appears to be alone. This time, he offers Doctor his hand and feigns a degree of warmth while offering him a seat. Doctor sits cautiously and perches on the edge of the deep, leather lounge chair in which he is sure he would feel uncomfortably vulnerable if he were to take full advantage. Da Costa is dressed in a crisp white shirt and blue chinos. Once again, Doctor is made to feel inferior even though the clothes he is wearing are new and combined with his imposing stature, he cuts an impressive figure to the casual observer.

Da Costa, who already knows of Hlengiwe's getaway, opens cautiously. He knows he will shortly have to flee Southern Africa because the events of the last few days and especially the murder of Mozambican policemen are certainly going to lead to his arrest. However, he needs to keep Doctor in suspense for a bit longer. He starts by probing Doctor's willingness to take money in return for his silence. He quickly concludes that this awkward journalist is not in the market. Of his two weaknesses, Hlengiwe is his best chance so long as Doctor believes she is still his hostage. Actually, he no longer really cares about Doctor and is only motivated by the desire to take others down with him.

Da Costa admits that he will soon be on his way out of the country and he just needs Doctor's silence for a few days. He decides to go for broke by tantalising Doctor. A senior figure in the South African government has been taking a monthly payment from his company for the last year in return for contracts servicing the embryonic oil and gas exploration activity offshore. The story will make his association with Lucas and Pardon seem trivial. If Doctor cooperates, he will give him the full story in a few days' time. In the meantime, he can arrange for Hlengiwe to be released unharmed.

At that moment, Doctor's phone rings. It is a Mozambican number. He picks up and hears Hlengiwe's voice. At first, he does not understand but she quickly makes it clear that she has escaped and then been rescued. She is unharmed and just very anxious about him. Doctor reassures her and asks her to call him back in five minutes.

Doctor contains his joy for a little longer. He stands up and tells Da Costa that he will think about his offer. He leaves rapidly half expecting to be intercepted by Da Costa's men.

Once out of the hotel he walks briskly along the sea front waiting for Hlengiwe to call back. His emotions are all over the place; joy, relief and continuing fear are all bubbling to the surface.

Hlengiwe calls back some twenty minutes later. Her composure is gone and she weeps. In between sobs she manages to tell him a little more about her ordeal. Slowly the crying subsides and she mentions that she plans to drive south to Maputo in the morning to re-join him. Doctor is not happy with this idea and promises to meet her in XaiXai in the next few hours although he is not sure how he will get there.

Doctor calls Du Toit and he agrees, readily, to drive him to XaiXai. He needs to liaise with the local team and lead a search of the farmhouse so leaving a few hours earlier is not a big inconvenience for him. Besides he has developed a liking for Doctor and hopes that he can learn more about Da Costa's business dealings on the two-hour journey.

As it turns out, Doctor sleeps for most of the journey. On the way, their car is stopped at a police roadblock. Du Toit flashes his badge and the officer peering into the car is suddenly very courteous and aborts his normal routine designed to extract a small bribe from the driver. It is the early hours of the morning when they arrive but Hlengiwe is still at the police headquarters and wide awake as the adrenalin in her body has yet to dissipate. She rushes to greet Doctor and the couple embrace each other in a way that threatens to weld them together.

Du Toit drives the three of them to a small hotel in town. Doctor and Hlengiwe collapse into their bed, he holding her tightly to him and they quickly fall into a deep sleep.

When they eventually emerge in the middle of the morning, Du Toit has long checked out. He has already arranged for Hlengiwe's car to be driven round to the hotel. The couple are mostly silent; shocked still and disbelieving of the events of the last couple of days. A distance opens up between them. Hlengiwe mentions that she needs to return home and get back to work. She offers to leave the car and take a bus back to Mbombela. Doctor has promised Du Toit he will not leave for another day or two so after some half-hearted protests about the car, he agrees that it would be very useful to have some wheels. In return, he offers her his cell phone; her own was taken when she was abducted. This makes no sense to either of them. They take a walk and Doctor outlines his thoughts for how he will continue the investigation. They buy a cheap cell phone that Hlengiwe can use until she gets back home and get a proper replacement. Doctor will collect her things from the guest house in Maputo before he heads home in a few days.

At the bus station, Doctor buys Hlengiwe a ticket to Maputo where she can connect with the Intercape bus and the five-hour trip to Mbombela. The local bus is due to leave in less than an hour. They grab a coffee and talk awkwardly. Then it is time to say goodbye. They kiss and hold each other but Hlengiwe seems distracted and uncertain. Doctor is confused and feels that their new relationship is in crisis.

After she has gone, Doctor feels an emptiness that is worse than that he experienced when he thought she might be dead. He texts her new phone to let he know he is thinking of her. She does not reply.

Doctor calls Du Toit and arranges to meet him for dinner that evening when he expects to be back from the farmhouse. He starts work on his next article exposing the XaiXai Investments story and, finding it hard to organise his thoughts, he calls his editor to brief him. The editor is very happy with this new and very intimate angle on the murder and kidnap of Mozambican policemen that has been on the wires during the morning. He does not pass comment on the wisdom of taking a girlfriend on this trip. The possibility of an even bigger corruption story is making his mouth water. Doctor promises to pen a short breaking news piece to be posted online before the end of the day, focusing on the murder of the policemen, and a longer piece for The Sunday Times.

The moment his editor hangs up, Doctor receives a new call. It is Da Costa. He starts by hoping that his girlfriend is recovering from her ordeal and stressing that she was treated well while in his care. Doctor is non-committal. Da Costa has information about the whereabouts of the two surviving policemen from the previous nights failed rescue mission. Maybe Doctor can use that information. He thanks Doctor sarcastically for his help and rings off abruptly.

Doctor calls Du Toit with the information he has just received. Du Toit is less impressed than he had hoped since the two men have just, minutes earlier, walked into the XaiXai Police Station.

Next Doctor calls Pardon and asks after Lucas. Is he available to talk? She hands her phone to her husband. Lucas is still recovering from the shock of having his cars and other assets confiscated as promised by his visitor of the previous day. He can barely bring himself to talk.

Doctor mentions that he has information involving a more senior figure in the National Government. Can Lucas help him? Lucas is not about to say anything on the phone but he agrees to talk to Doctor again when he returns to Mpumalanga.

Chapter 21
Recollection

Junior Khumalo is alone at home in Centurion. His wife, Pumza, is visiting family in Kwa Zulu Natal. The housekeeper has brought him breakfast in his study and The Sunday Times is awaiting his attention on the desk. The headline grabs his attention; "Mozambican Police Die in XaiXai Shoot Out." In smaller print, Doctor Lukhele is credited with the piece. How has Doctor travelled from the South Johannesburg school system to be on point for the violence in XaiXai? More worryingly, is this violence linked to his Mozambican associates? Until now he had not noticed the missed call from Da Costa in the early hours. He hits the call back but it goes straight to voicemail.

It takes Junior a few more seconds finally to dredge up the memory of the Sunday afternoon at the Zoo Lake in 1976 and the Doctor Lukhele that saved him from his temper that day. He thinks that he remembers that Khumalo, whom he met only once, was one of the comrades who died while in detention in John Vorster Square during the Soweto uprising. It seems unlikely that the Doctor who is a journalist is not linked. He calls one of his oldest friends, a veteran of the struggle, who remembers that Doctor Lukhele had a girlfriend. It was he who had delivered the bad news to the despairing girl but he couldn't remember her name. She was living in Alex at the time. From the furthest reaches of his memory, Junior remembers the beautiful girl at the Zoo Lake and somehow, he retrieves it; the name of the girl was Lefa.

As the recollection comes into focus, Junior is immersed in a cold sweat. He revisits the period in June 1976 when, like many of his comrades, he was arrested, interrogated and tortured in John Vorster Square. For years he has suffered from nightmares while successfully suppressing the detail of those long terrifying hours and the culminating, wretched betrayal that led to his release and changed the course of his life. He had expected to die but he had not and, of course, he knew exactly why. A new wave of the cold sweat engulfed him.

Chapter 22
Dawn Raid

The staff of the Provincial Administration are still in shock after the early morning raid on their offices. Joy is busy helping one of the Hawk team. She has driven with him to the archive building a couple of kilometres up the hill in Rocky's Drift. Neither her colleagues, nor the Hawk team, are aware that it is her whistleblowing that has triggered the events of the last few days. Nevertheless, she is nervous that her role will be exposed. They have already sampled a number of recent claims still in the main filing system and now they are doing the same with the older claims that were carefully archived by Joy and her predecessor. In Pretoria, a group of auditors are going through the sampled claims looking for the tell-tale signs of wrongdoing. A quick analysis of the claims system suggests the average employee claim is about one thousand rand per month. The samples they have taken include some of these low value claims but the focus of the team is on claims over five thousand. Then they are looking for lines in the claims that are not supported by a receipt or invoice. These are not difficult to spot and it is a continual surprise that employees think they can get away with such easily detected fraud. They have isolated all the claims of Lucas and April for the last 2 years and all the claims approved by Lucas in the same period. Any claim that looks questionable is subject to a more detailed investigation and other claims of the employee concerned are pulled from the records for scrutiny.

A separate team is working with a Procurement specialist to sample contracts from all the departments with a special focus on those endorsed by Lucas.

Three senior Hawks are each interviewing one of the Department Heads in the Provincial Administration in the expectation that the corruption they are uncovering probably goes to the top.

Mkhize arrives and his three senior interrogators adjourn to update him on their questioning so far. The Department Heads have been able to describe the controls in place in their organisations and are adamant, of course, that there is no systematic corruption to be found. The sampling of employee expenses and contracts is beginning to paint a different picture.

Thabo Mkhize decides he needs to talk to Lucas's boss, a Member of Executive Council who herself reports to the Provincial Premier. Mrs Pretty Mthembu is a formidable looking woman who enters the meeting room that Thabo has commandeered with all the confidence that she can muster. Nevertheless, her breathlessness suggests that she is more nervous about this interview than she would like him to think.

Thabo begins by asking Pretty if she is aware of the reason for his team's presence in the building. She is, of course, fully briefed on the background to Lucas's fraud charges and it was her that handled his suspension pending the outcome of his trial. Is she aware of the relationship between Lucas and April? Pretty says that she only became aware of an alleged affair between her two employees after April's murder. She has already been interviewed by the police murder investigation team on that matter.

A knock on the glass door of the glass meeting room and a young Hawk with a bundle of contract papers in her hand enters the room. Thabo hustles her out again and they have a whispered conversation in the corridor before he re-enters with the papers.

The contract that he places on the table between him and Pretty is a high value contract for consultancy services that had been endorsed by the MEC herself. The consultancy is a locally based company which Thabo has not heard of. The contract is signed by the Administration's Procurement Director. The second signature on the contract, that of the Consultancy's CEO is a name that he had not immediately recognised. His colleague has just explained that it is the wife of a National Government minister, Junior Khumalo.

Chapter 23
Royal Visit

Hlengiwe is at home with her mother and trying to explain the last few days to her without scaring her too much. Her mother is not easily fooled and realises she has been through a life-threatening experience. She tells Hlengiwe that she was foolish to accompany Doctor on the hazardous trip and though she knows that her mother is right it is not really what she wants hear. She fights the angry reaction which frequently ended discussions with her mother as a rebellious teenager. Nevertheless, home comforts and her mother's listening ear eventually restore a sense of perspective. She is alive and back in South Africa. She has no reason to fear Da Costa who anyway was only using her as a bargaining chip. His time for bargaining is over and escape is his first priority.

Hlengiwe's mother, seeing her daughter struggle with the trauma of the last few days, leaves the room for a few minutes before returning with a shoe box full of family photographs; black and white and faded colour memories of Hlengiwe's childhood and more interestingly of aunts and uncles and cousins barely remembered. In the past, Hlengiwe would badger her mother to bring out the battered box and bring the photographs to life with her stories.

Hlengiwe readily submits to what she knows will be an hour or two of random but always interesting memories embroidered by her mother and involving alternately giggles and tears.

One of the black and white photographs catches Hlengiwe's attention. It shows her grandparents on her mother's side. They are standing stiffly, in their church clothes, outside the old railway station at Mataffin and behind them is a banner "Nelspruit Welcomes the Royal Family". The faded pencil writing on the back of the print suggests the photograph was taken in 1947. On one side of the station entrance, there is a crowd of people waving the flags of Great Britain and the old Union of South Africa. On the other side there is a welcoming party of entirely white citizens in their specially purchased finery and a Rolls-Royce with its uniformed driver standing by. Hlengiwe's mother recalls that the Rolls-Royce belonged to the owner of the citrus farm at Mataffin on which her parents were employed. They had been brought up in a rural location called Moremela, a day's walk, in those days, from the nearest dorp of Graskop. The people were mostly of BaPedi heritage. Moremela was baking hot in summer and intensely cold for a few weeks in winter. There was little work and most families subsisted from their small holding of goats and a hectare or so of mielie. The young couple had heard about work on the citrus farms near Nelspruit and had decided to make their life there after they married. They were a handsome, if threadbare, couple in the photograph. Hlengiwe remembers her doting grandparents when they were already elderly. Their faces were lined as testament to the constant struggle that was their lives; the Apartheid system was designed precisely to keep them in poverty, working six long days every week for subsistence wages, and they rarely travelled more than a few miles from their adopted home except perhaps for a funeral in their home location.

Hlengiwe remembers the family picnics that they organised on Sunday afternoons, after church, in summer. These would take place at the foot of a granite kopje that was a short walk from their one-roomed house on the farm. The children would scramble to the top of the rock, invariably grazing their knees, while adults prepared tea and mielie pap with tamatie sauce. Occasionally, a small herd of buck would stare curiously before leaping into the long grass at the sound of a child's scream. Sometimes a snake would sidewind away from the children as they moved carelessly over its sunbathing territory. Always, the crickets would provide a background chorus that was etched into Hlengiwe's subconscious.

The picnics would end as dusk encroached and the new week would be preceded by a deep, carefree sleep that Hlengiwe rarely replicated these days.

The uncomplicated contentment that she felt then reminds her of her new, recently neglected lover.

Later, Hlengiwe would visit a favourite cousin with Doctor; a cousin who then sported grazed knees after the picnic kopje climbs. Doctor would try and fail to put himself alongside the cousins on those childhood Sundays and to share the laughter into which they would dissolve. He did succeed in understanding, at least a little, why her eyes were always so immutably childlike as if fixed in a simpler, happy time.

Hlengiwe calls Doctor for the first time since they parted. She is sorry that she left him hanging but she needed some time to process everything that happened including the feelings she has for Doctor which she realises have deepened.

Hlengiwe's priority now is to organise her house move.

Chapter 24
Conflict of Interest

Thabo Mkhize waits for Pretty to break the silence. The consultancy contract that he has confronted her with is not so exceptional. But the fact that there appears to be links to a family member of a senior government minister is worthy of some further investigation.

Eventually Pretty can bear the silence no longer. What exactly does Thabo see in this contract that is eluding her? He asks her whether she met Pumza Khumalo during the contract negotiations and what she knows of Pumza.

Pretty thinks back to the day of the bid presentations. The three bidders shortlisted had come to pitch for the provision of consultancy services to Lucas's department. The Department was struggling to ensure that farmland continued to be productive after transfer to local clans in successful land restitution claims. The contractor was to provide training and promote skills transfer for farm managers and their workers during the period of transition to new ownership. The original concept of having compensated landowners provide that service was not working out and, increasingly, acreages were being left fallow.

The shortlisted bidders in turn made a thirty-minute pitch followed by questions from Lucas's team. Pretty had been invited to attend because of the political importance of the initiative. She had toyed with the idea of sending her deputy but Lucas had met with her a few days earlier and suggested that her presence would be very helpful. During the meeting, Lucas had summarised the bid evaluations and mentioned that he had already formed a preference for the bid from Hadida Agri Solutions. The bid was not the cheapest and Hadida was a relatively new player but they were proposing a radical new approach which Lucas felt would play very well with the public. Finally, Lucas mentioned that Hadida's CEO was Pumza Khumalo who happened to be the wife of Junior Khumalo, the prominent government minister. Pretty was immediately alert to the potential concerns raised by awarding the contract to Pumza's company and she asked Lucas to provide her with a more detailed briefing before the presentations. As it happened, Lucas had not come back to her but the same afternoon, she had received a call from none other than Pumza Khumalo herself. Pumza had been charming and invited Pretty to join her for a few days at the Cape Grace Hotel during the Cape Town Jazz Festival last March. Pretty had enjoyed the stay very much and had got to know Pumza quite well. Pumza had picked up the tab for all her expenses during the trip and had even taken her shopping.

Pretty does not share much of this with Thabo but she did admit that she had spoken to Pumza before the contract award while being emphatic that Pumza's connections had not in any way influenced the outcome of the bidding process. She had received and accepted the recommendation from Lucas, as was normal.

Thabo has Pretty's expense claims from the recent months summarised in a spreadsheet on his laptop. He notes there is a four-day trip to Cape Town in March during which Pretty had racked up close to twenty thousand rand including her flights, three nights in a five-star hotel and some fancy dinners. There is nothing immediately to link it to Pumza nor to Hadida. The purpose of the trip is given as "Meetings with Cape Province Officials".

Thabo's well-honed instincts kick in and he asks Pretty to talk him through the trip and the meetings she attended. Pretty becomes flustered and claims to have forgotten. She will have to check her diary. While she is checking her smartphone, Thabo, following his hunch, checks the last four digits of the credit card used to pay the Cape Grace bill, and notices that they do not tally with the business credit card that Pretty normally uses.

Pretty surfaces from her diary check to confirm a meeting with her Western Cape counterpart on the first day of her Cape Town visit. Thabo asks her to go on. Pretty is now looking very flushed and is unable to offer any further information. The remaining days of the trip were apparently a blank.

Thabo asks her if she can produce the credit card that is referenced on the hotel bill. She cannot. She is sure that she used her business expenses card.

Thabo, following his hunch, suggests that he will find that the credit card belongs to Pumza Kumalo. Pretty is by now barely suppressing a blind panic. She had expected that the interview would focus on the conduct of Lucas and that she would be able to incriminate him without revealing her own misdemeanours. Finally, she gets hold of herself just long enough to admit in a faltering voice that the bill was paid for by Pumza. Thabo leaves the room to return, minutes later with two uniformed officers. Pretty is arrested and led out of the building to a waiting car. A few minutes later she is being charged with fraud and bailed to appear in court the following morning. Thabo will need a bit more time to investigate the full extent of the corruption but for now he feels he has had a good afternoon.

Chapter 25
June 1976

Junior was heading towards Orlando in his battered, but prized, 1962, pale blue, Ford Anglia. He was alone. A car full of young black men would too easily attract the suspicion of police at the road blocks he was expecting. The sense of freedom that he had whenever he drove himself made him feel warm and self-satisfied. His life as an ANC member and activist brought him into contact with some mid-ranking cadre members, mostly ten years older than himself. To Junior they seemed overly cautious and reluctant to back the recent student unrest in the townships. Even after the shootings of June 16th, they were mostly trying to keep their people calm and discourage overreaction. Junior felt that they had an opportunity now to turn the townships into no-go zones for the security forces. He and several others had been ordered to go to Orlando to report on the planned demonstrations and to do what they could to keep things peaceful. On the route out of Joburg, he counted dozens of buses carrying young people towards the southern townships.

Junior Khumalo had been born into a middle-class family. His father was a school teacher in a township near Potchefstroom. He had one sister, two years older. He had been lucky enough to study to standard ten and matriculate. This made him a rarity alongside most of his peers who mostly left school by standard eight or earlier.

Junior's father had wanted him to carry on his education in Swaziland where his sister was training to be a nurse. Father had been saving for years to afford the fees that would allow his children to get one small step ahead of the apartheid system.

Junior has other ideas. He had heard that there was money to be made in Johannesburg and in the New Year of 1973 he had headed for the big city, excited but uncertain what he would find. He quickly got a job as a trainee motor mechanic and he learnt fast so that his boss would often ask him to repair the cars that had stubborn problems his colleagues had failed to fix. The Anglia that he was now driving was one such case and the white owner had decided to sell it for scrap before Junior got his hands on it and gave it a new lease of life.

About six months after his arrival in Johannesburg, he started attending meetings held secretly by a small group of ANC and Communist Party activists who has gone underground more than a dozen years earlier when the organisations were banned. He had heard about the meetings from his boss who was Jewish and still secretly a member of the Communist Party. He had given up his political activities in order to run his business, raise his family and keep out of trouble. Like many people, pragmatism trumped idealism. In the smart Junior, he saw the possibility of activism by proxy.

Junior had never really thought much about politics and his parents had always shielded him from the worst aspects of the system. Even the meetings he attended did not really inspire him. He did see, however, that there was a chance to become somebody by making himself useful to the cadres who was at constant risk of arrest if exposed. His early missions were straightforward but gave him a sense of excitement missing from the rest of his life. He spent his weekends shadowing people that the ANC were interested in or checking out for some reason. The Party had given him a small loan for the Ford Anglia and, with this mobility, his usefulness increased.

In early June 1976, Junior was shadowing a white scientist who had shown interest in the ANC but had also aroused suspicion because his military experience and his privileged upbringing suggested that he might be a spy. One Sunday he had followed the scientist and his wife to the Zoo Lake and it was here that he had intervened on behalf of a courting couple who were being harassed by a policeman. The intervention had grown heated and he had lost his temper. Fortunately, the young man, on whose behalf Junior had intervened, restrained him and the confrontation came to nothing. He did however make a mental note of the young Doctor Lukhele that had introduced himself after the incident.

Junior arrived in Orlando via a circuitous route that he reckoned, correctly, would avoid the police road blocks. He left his car in a quiet spot, shaded from the winter sunshine, some way from the stadium where he expected to find the main demonstration that he been tasked to monitor. As he walked away from his parked car, he noticed a white Ford Cortina coasting to a halt just a short distance up the road. He realised immediately that the two men that got out could only be policemen. They were both dressed in khaki slacks and brilliant white, short sleeved shirts. More importantly, they were the only whites not in uniform in this township location.

Junior tried to look casual and sauntered along the deserted dusty road for a minute or two cursing his decision to park out of sight of others. The two plain clothes men kept their distance though their attempt at a saunter was more of a military slow march. Junior broke into a jog. The men went to a quick march without closing. Junior ran. The men shouted out for him to stop and drew pistols.

Junior did not stop. Several shots followed him. Then a sharp pain in his leg and a fall to the ground. Seconds later there was a powerful kick to the side of his head. Then nothing.

He came around in a dark room. A cell obviously. His leg was strapped with a tourniquet. His trouser was soaked in blood. He could feel a swelling on his left temple that was painful to the touch.

Chapter 26
Back to The Lowveld

Doctor is on his way back to South Africa. Hlengiwe's Golf is making easy work of the highway to the border from Maputo. The drive from XaiXai to Maputo had taken longer than it should because of road works. Now he is confident of arriving in Kabokweni by late afternoon. He calls his aunt and agrees to pick her up in White River when she finishes work.

The day is hot again and still no sign of the rain. At the border, he is waved through the Mozambican side and it takes only a few minutes to walk through the passport control on the South African side. There is a long queue for foreigners many of whom have already crossed other borders on the route south.

Doctor makes a call to Lucas, who sounds like a nervous wreck, and they agree to meet the following morning at his home since he is effectively under house arrest having had his cars confiscated.

Back on the road, the landscape grows towards the now familiar Lowveld hills and their winter khaki lawns thirsting for the rain which will transform them into lush green. The high escarpment beyond is grey in the haze. Doctor picks up a young man from Swaziland who is heading to Johannesburg to look for work; the latest in successive generations of migrant workers that have felt the magnetic pull of the City of Gold, Egoli. They chat lightly until the young man is dropped off in Mbombela, the migrant to continue west, while Doctor heads the short distance north to pick up his aunt.

The radio news leads on the latest round of electricity load shedding, the root cause of which is corruption in government and the leadership of the state-owned electricity company, Eskom. The public is rapidly becoming expert in the black art of boiler tube maintenance and the consequences of neglect. A whole new vocabulary has evolved to frame the story. Doctor is not sure whether to laugh or cry at the prospect of the rich vein of stories, not far from the surface, that he can mine for the foreseeable future. He has a feeling that his current investigation will break through into the deeper seam of corruption that is undermining the potential of his beloved country. Lucas, perhaps, holds the key.

At White River, his Aunt Funi is waiting for Doctor at the Pick 'n Pay. She is surprised when his tall frame appears from the unrecognized Golf and goes immediately into her mother hen routine that has become the norm for their meetings. Doctor gives her a sanitized version of the last few days as they drive the remaining short distance to Kabokweni. Funi's clucking reaches a crescendo before he drops her off at home and promises to return for supper. Then he heads urgently to Hlengiwe to return her car and reassure himself that they are alright.

Reassurance comes rapidly as Hlengiwe rushes out to embrace him.

Chapter 27
Betrayal

Junior's body clock told him that it must be the middle of the night when he was dragged from his brightly lit cell and taken to a stark, windowless room which would be the scene of his interrogation over the next few days. Sometimes he was allowed to sit opposite his interrogator separated by a scrubbed wooden desk that was stained with the rings of coffee mugs and cigarette burns. Mostly he was forced to stand with his hands cuffed. The bullet wound in his leg remained untreated. It was not painful and the tourniquet was effective in stopping the bleeding although he was worried about the numbness in his foot especially when he was sitting. The man opposite him was in plain clothes. He stared contemptuously at Junior and chain smoked. For hours, Junior said nothing in response to the man's questions. Then Plain Clothes left and two uniforms entered. They moved him to a corner of the room underneath a shower head. He was drenched in cold water and left alone for several hours. He had relieved himself while the shower was running to avoid a more obvious embarrassment. He was getting very hungry. The shower water had taken the edge off his thirst. The unheated room and the clinging wet clothes triggered a descent into delirious hypothermia.

The Plain Clothes returned and the questioning resumed. The questioning was focused on who he knew and what he knew about ANC sabotage plans. The people he knew were unimportant political cadres. Sabotage was run by uMkhonto we Sizwe, the military wing of the ANC, about which he knew nothing.

The shivering Junior still managed to say nothing. A cigarette was offered. Junior had never smoked. Some hot, milky, sweet tea brought some relief and the interrogation became a little friendlier for a while.

An idea came into his head driven by the desire to sleep and for warmth. He invented a plan to blow up a cooling tower at the power station near Jan Smuts airport. He mentioned that a young Swazi from the Eastern Transvaal was the bomb maker. He thought his name was Doctor. He did not really expect they would take him very seriously and, anyway, the Doctor he had met was hardly a credible terrorist. Surely. He thought he was just buying time.

Junior was given some hot oats and allowed a few hours of sleep, naked, under a coarse blanket. Gradually his body temperature recovered. A doctor came and looked at his wound. The bullet had gone in and out. The wound was dressed and the tourniquet removed. An unexplained injection in Junior's buttock completed the treatment.

Meanwhile, unknown to Junior Khumalo, a few metres away, in the interrogation room he had just survived, the almost blameless Doctor was living his last few painful hours, ignorant of the fact that he had fathered the eponymous child who would become Junior's nemesis.

Chapter 28
Smoking Gun

Lucas greets Doctor at his front door. He is unshaven and has obviously not slept much in recent nights.

Pardon has gone to her sister's home in Johannesburg. The pain of seeing the unfaithful, discredited Lucas every hour of the day is too much for her. Her home no longer seems like a home; just an oversized house that feels cold and uninviting.

The two men go through the house onto the stoep that overlooks the golf course. Their footsteps echo coldly in the empty house. A golf buggy drives past beyond the swimming pool and the manicured garden, sputtering and lurching over the rough in which the driver's ball is lost. His clubs rattle metallically in the bag strapped to the back of the buggy. A sarcastic shout of encouragement comes from the golfer's partner who is smugly on the fairway. A lourie flies silently between trees at the edge of the garden; its crimson flight feathers drawing attention to its presence.

The housekeeper and the gardener have apparently been let go. There are already weeds in between the terracotta bricks paving the pool surrounds and little ant heaps sprouting up in the lawn. A green algae bloom is taking hold of the once sparking pool.

Lucas offers his visitor some chilled water and volunteers an update on his current situation. His attorney has been working with him to prepare a plea of mitigation when his case comes up in the High Court in a few months' time. The attorney has advised him to offer to turn state witness in return for a lenient sentence or just possibly immunity from prosecution. So far, the Hawks have not suggested that.

Doctor listens sympathetically and allows Lucas plenty of time before he moves on to ask about the information he has suggesting that a government minister might be at the centre of the web of corruption which is emerging. Lucas offers to provide some relevant information but he wants some money in return.

Doctor calls his editor at the Sunday Times who is quick to offer an amount that probably equates only to a month of Lucas's honestly earned salary. Lucas agrees equally quickly providing he gets the money in cash. Doctor is a bit surprised that the deal is so easy to make but guesses that he had some emergency cash stashed in the house but that is already running low or maybe Pardon has taken it with her. The editor promises to transfer the money to Doctor's account immediately so that he can draw the amount at an ATM and pay Lucas.

Lucas retells the story that he had shared with Captain Thabo Mkhize and the role of Mrs. Pumza Khumalo. He reveals that Pumza is the wife of Junior and checks his phone for her cell phone number and e-mail address. The trail that leads to national government is warming up. Lucas, seemingly, has no knowledge of the oil & gas service contracts that XaiXai have won and which Doctor's instinct tells him involve Junior Khumalo.

Lucas's voice is replaced by a mellifluous Cape Robin and its *"wur de wur"*. Its mate responds from a little further away. To Doctor, it sounds like they are asking each other "what 're you doing?" They may well ask, he thinks.

Doctor and Lucas leave the house together and head for Hazyview where Doctor is unable to draw the agreed amount of cash from an ATM as it exceeds his very modest daily limit. He draws a thousand rand and hands it to Lucas. In the branch, Doctor is able to draw the full amount on production of his ID card. Lucas relaxes visibly and take his leave, meaning to find his own way home. Before that he wants to buy some basic supplies to keep himself fed for the next week or so. They agree to stay in touch and wish each other luck. Doctor wonders why he feels any sympathy for Lucas; perhaps, he thinks, because he sees some similarities between his addiction and Lucas's inability to resist the temptation of easy money and a lifestyle that he could only have dreamed of as a child.

Chapter 29
Closing In

Captain Thabo Mkhize arrives, unannounced, at the home of Minister Junior Khumalo. Thabo asks for Pumza Khumalo. The policeman outside the gate, having checked Thabo's ID, calls the housekeeper. Neither Pumza nor the Minister are at home. Pumza is still at her childhood home in Kwa Zulu Natal. Thabo leaves his card at the gate and ask the housekeeper to get her madam to call him as soon as possible.

Pumza calls Thabo five minutes later while he is still sitting in his car parked outside the Khumalo residence. He introduces himself and mentions that he is investigating some irregularities in a provincial administration. His team have sampled some contracts that have been awarded recently. He would like to discuss her experience of the contract bidding process that she was recently involved in. Pumza reacts coolly but agrees to meet him when she gets home in two days' time. She does not mention that she has already been in contact with Pretty and is quietly polishing her story which will effectively distance her from the corrupt Provincial officials. She has discussed none of this with Junior.

Chapter 30
Double Agent

Junior awoke, still naked but warm enough under the coarse blanket. He began to piece together the detail of his interrogation. He realised with horror that his desperate invention would likely lead to the arrest or worse of the young man he had met at the Zoo Lake. He could only hope that some piece of good fortune or bureaucratic incompetence would prevent his betrayal from having any consequences.

After a couple of hours of fretting, the cell door opened. Some prison clothes were tossed onto his bunk by a faceless warder. A few minutes later a fully clothed, barefoot, Junior was marched to a new interrogation room; this time with a window that looked out over the older parts of Johannesburg. He guessed he was on the 6th floor or higher; the view across the city and her southern suburbs was unrestricted and he could see the yellow gold mining tailings heaps to the east of the city if he peered to his left. Cars, busses and trucks sped along the elevated highway in the foreground. To his right and just out of sight, a steam locomotive gave a long, shrill whistle as it pulled out of Park Station. The cloudless sky was a pale, winter blue. The staccato sound of a typewriter filtered into the room from across the passageway.

Plain Clothes entered followed by a shorter man dressed in an ill-fitting suit and a tie with a small, tight knot that was several inches below the open collar of his creased shirt. His face was put into soft focus by a couple of days growth of salt and pepper stubble. He looked short of sleep. He also looked incongruously kindly, Junior thought. The two white men sat and invited Junior, who was still standing at the window, to do the same. Plain

Clothes, forgetfully offering Junior an unwanted cigarette, explained that his colleague was from the Bureau of State Security. Given Junior's helpful attitude during their last "meeting", Plain Clothes thought he might be interested in a proposal. The man from BOSS eyed him intently apparently trying to judge the character of this young man. Junior realised that his earlier thinking was hopelessly optimistic and the invented information he had volunteered under interrogation had been taken seriously.

The BOSS officer mentioned that some of Junior's fellow cadres were already making their way into exile in Angola, Mozambique and Zambia since the clamp down following the Soweto uprising. Once released, he should talk up his arrest and subsequent treatment and persuade his ANC superiors to send him into exile also. Then he would be contacted by a local agent to whom he should report comings and goings in whichever training camp he ended up in. In return for his agreement he would be let go and left unmolested. Junior knew that it was not necessary to ask about what might happen if he did not agree. He also knew now, after the last few hours, that he was not made of the stuff of a hero who could die under interrogation. He was disappointed in himself but not that surprised. He had occasionally wondered how he would cope under fire and now he seemed to have the answer.

There was little more detail in the proposal; only that failure to follow through once in exile would lead to Junior's exposure as a traitor. No further explanation was required.

Junior was taken back to his cell and after a short wait led out to a prison van. Later, after a short drive, he was unceremoniously dumped next to the road and by a piece of wasteland that turned out to be considerately close to Alexandra. After getting his bearings, he was able to limp home and report back to his colleagues. His sanitised version of his experiences since the Saturday in Orlando were suitably convincing and his standing amongst the cadres rose accordingly. After a further few days he was heading towards the border with Botswana. He travelled in a Kombi with a dozen migrant mineworkers returning home. His forged papers enabled him to pass as a Botswana National with a work permit for the East Rand Gold Mines. From Botswana he made his way, with two other escaping cadres to Zambia where he spent the next fourteen years except for a year's political training in Havana.

Over these years, Junior's steady leak of information would be instrumental in the assassination of several prominent ANC leaders. He rose through the ranks of the ANC in exile and was highly valued as an administrator. He came to be Head of Logistics for the ANC in Zambia and had access to all personnel movements which made his task very straightforward. He managed to live with his actions because it was clear to him that the ANC would eventually succeed in its mission. His actions, he rationalised to himself, were merely delaying the inevitable.

Chapter 31
Lucky Men

Doctor is busy installing the washing machine in the laundry room of Hlengiwe's new house. Plumbing is not really his strong point but the instructions make it look easy enough and although his knuckles are bleeding after the unfamiliar wrench slipped as he tightened a joint, he is happy to be doing something of a domestic nature that is helpful to Hlengiwe. She in turn is running from room to room unpacking some of the things she brought from her mother's home and meeting deliveries of some new furniture that she has bought to make her new home the special place she hopes it will be. Her Mother who will share the house with her is still in Kabokweni cleaning the empty house that she has lived in for thirty years and saying a tearful goodbye to her neighbours.

Doctor's phone rings and it is his editor. He explains that he has been approached by the Hawks who are interested in Doctor's investigation. They have requested full disclosure from Doctor of his investigation to date and the leads he is following up. Doctor is surprised that the Hawks think that he knows more than they do but he agrees with his editor that cooperation is key and maybe even helpful in giving him the inside track to the centre of the web of corruption that he is untangling. The only caveat is that the Hawks have asked for a hold on further publication until they are sure that the key arrests have been made. Doctor can expect a call in the next hour or two. As a by the way, before cutting the call, the editor casually mentions that Doctor is to be offered a staff contract with the paper.

In the event, it is less than fifteen minutes before Captain Thabo Mkhize calls and coolly suggests meeting up. Thabo is in

Mbombela after his trip home to Gauteng. Doctor suggests his favourite coffee shop and heads there after quickly updating Hlengiwe on the way out. He is relegated to his faithful Polo again but the gracefully ageing car seems happy to be reunited with her owner and the engine purrs softly on the short trip into town. Doctor is strangely unsettled by the editor's apparent afterthought. The Sunday Times is his dream job but he has grown accustomed to the independent life of a freelance and now that it is beginning to pay him proper money, he is not sure he wants to change.

Thabo is at the coffee shop already and has taken a seat in a booth that gives the two men some privacy. Thabo gets up and shakes Doctor's hand in a firm grip suggestive of a warm nature. The two men are a similar age and they start by giving each other a short biography. Thabo's story is quite different from his own; Doctor listens as the policeman talks of an affluent upbringing in a green suburb of Johannesburg and entrepreneurial parents who could afford a university education for their only child. Although it would be easy for Thabo to sound boastful and vain, in fact he comes over as a modest man who knows that he was born lucky. Doctor sketches out his Soweto upbringing, his university and writing experience while missing out the messy alcoholic time that he prefers to forget. To Thabo, he sounds like a man who knows he has worked hard but still needed some luck to escape the poverty that his forebears could not.

The Hawk explains to Doctor that, following April Coetzee's murder, his team have uncovered some important but relatively low-level corruption and fraud in the Provincial Administration some of which corroborates Doctor's Sunday Times exposé. The leads he is investigating now has taken him to the wife of a government minister. He is fairly sure the minister himself is involved but he has yet to uncover evidence to confirm that. Doctor has yet to follow up on the tip off he got from Da Costa and he wonders for a moment whether to share it. The Hawk, seeing the hesitation, shares a bit more detail including Pretty's expenses fraud and the link to the contract award for Pumza's consulting business. Doctor is still unimpressed. He knows all this from his meeting with Lucas. Thabo goes on to explain that he is meeting the minister's wife in a day or so and he is hoping for some new information to help him overcome her first line of defence and claims of innocence.

Doctor, deciding to open up, goes over some of the ground that Thabo has already gleaned from the Sunday Times front page splash on the XaiXai shootings. The role of Da Costa and his associates is familiar until he gets to illegal payments related to the Oil & Gas Services contracts that Da Costa had mentioned in his last call to Doctor. Thabo makes the same connection that Doctor had made during his discussion with Lucas. The government minister might just be the husband of Pumza Khumalo.

Chapter 32
Graskop Clinic

Hlengiwe, her Mother and Doctor are together for the first time in Hlengiwe's new home. Hlengiwe is making supper for the three of them. While she is in the kitchen, her Mother is sharing her dim view of the ill-advised Maputo trip and in particular the danger that her daughter had been put in the way of. Doctor is sheepishly apologetic. There is a long, embarrassed silence before Mother launches into a childhood recollection; a violent incident that has lived with her since and which is now amplifying her instinctive protectiveness for her daughter.

She was visiting an Aunt in her parent's village in the Spring of 1976 when she got sick. Her Aunt treated her with hot honey and ginger water for a couple of days but she only got worse and the local midwife thought she might have pneumonia. Aunt and sick child caught the bus to the clinic in Graskop. The clinic had been set up by an Indian Muslim doctor for the benefit of the local, mainly rural, population who could not afford to attend the hospital in Nelspruit nor the fees charged by the local private doctors. They arrived at the clinic in the mid-morning and were told they would have to wait for at least two hours as the doctor had many patients to see. They had been in the busy waiting room for just a short while when they heard the roar of a convoy of police trucks approaching. Seconds later, a squad of policemen burst into the waiting room. A sergeant shouted orders in Afrikaans; telling the waiting patients to get out and declaring the clinic closed. As the frightened patients started to leave, a young policeman, apparently spooked by a sudden move from the small crowd, started hitting out indiscriminately with his sjambok. Several other officers joined in and Hlengiwe's Mother, hiding in the folds of her Aunt's skirt, was struck hard several times. An officer entered the room, now filled with panicked people trying to get out as quickly as possible. Ignoring the hubbub, he went straight to the consulting room and could be heard shouting at the doctor; suggesting a variety of unpleasant thoughts but most loudly, repeating several times, that he was a filthy communist. The doctor's gentle voice could be heard in a useless plead of innocence that fell on the deaf ears of the paranoid officer. By the time everybody was out of the clinic, the Doctor was being bundled into a police truck. Inside, the furniture and medical instruments were being smashed. Finally, two men put a heavy gauge chain and padlock to secure the front doors of the clinic. The ousted patients sat on the clinic stoep in shock and distress, nursing their bruises as the police drove away. That was the end of the clinic and the rumours that spread through the area suggested that the doctor had left for Europe a few weeks later. The girl's suspected pneumonia was never treated and it was several weeks before her aunt felt she was fit enough to travel back to Mataffin.

*

Hlengiwe's supper is ready. The three sit at the kitchen table and Mother leads with a prayer of thanks for the food. Doctor cleans his plate quickly and Hlengiwe does not have to persuade him to take a second helping of the spicy vegetable stew with rice that she has prepared in his honour. He is still feeling the hint of disapproval from Mother. For the time being, she is hiding the more important sense she has; that this Doctor might just be the right man for her precious daughter.

140

Chapter 33
Pumza Khumalo

Thabo has made an early start and is driving west again, back to Gauteng, for his meeting with Pumza Khumalo. He stops at the Alzu Petroport east of Middleburg for breakfast. A tourist bus has arrived a minute or two ahead of him and is disgorging its cargo of greying Japanese couples who are still chatting excitedly of their safari experience in the Kruger National Park. Thabo follows the group into the food court and watches as one couple heads to the ATM. The couple draw some money and are turning to re-join their companions when they are intercepted by two young men. The men appear to be suggesting a problem; pointing at the ATM and showing the Japanese a slip of paper apparently from the machine. The men are well dressed and their demeanour is friendly, not at all threatening. Nevertheless, Thabo is unconvinced and follows them from behind his sunglasses. The rapid-fire English of the smiling men is clearly confusing the tourists as they are guided gently back towards the machine. The men switch to sign language to try to persuade the man to offer his card to the machine for a second time. Now he has realised, rather late, that he is about to be the victim of a scam and turns away with his wife in tow. One of the scammers grabs him firmly by the elbow and tries to lead him back to the ATM. There are a cluster of people in the area but they seem oblivious of the developing incident. Thabo, who has been closing in, moves quickly and separates the would-be victim tourist from his assailant whose accomplice in turn moves to intervene. Thabo's training kicks in and he has the assailant handcuffed before the accomplice can finish his move. Instead, he makes a run for it leaving his friend in Thabo's custody. Two policemen arrive on the scene and Thabo is able to hand over his prisoner before being surrounded by effusive Japanese tourists who insist on buying him breakfast. Back on the road, he wonders whether they will remember South Africa for its wildlife, its criminal threat or the swift intervention of a hungry, plain clothes policeman.

Two hours later, arriving at the Khumalo residence, Thabo is waved through the motorised gates and swings round the front of the impressive contemporary house with its grey rendering, large smoked glass windows and downlighters. A pair of polished stainless-steel columns in the portico turn out to be expensive water features and their gentle splashing generates a helpful wave of calm in a Thabo anxious to make his breakthrough.

Pumza is waiting in her study and walks towards Thabo as he enters; greeting him stiffly and directing him to a chair in front of her desk. She retreats to her own chair and sits. Her posture is perfect, Thabo notices, and although he guesses she must be in her late forties she looks younger. She is immaculately dressed and exudes the kind of confidence he has become accustomed to when dealing with the new rich of the country who, so often, are the subjects of his investigations. He notices a framed photograph on the bookshelf behind her desk. Pumza and Junior are in a small, smiling group with former President Thabo Mbeki. An MBA Certificate from an American Business School also features on her trophy wall.

There is an exchange of business cards and Thabo again outlines his interest in Pumza's experience of the award process for the consultancy contract which her company has recently won with the Provincial Administration in Mpumalanga. Pumza sits back and launches into a well-rehearsed speech about the successful growth of Hadida under her leadership and summarises the

142

sectors that her company is targeting. Amongst several others, she mentions the increasingly important Oil & Gas sector in several countries in Southern Africa including Mozambique and Angola as well as its embryonic form in South Africa itself. Thabo is grateful for the opportunity to talk about that but keeps his powder dry for the moment as he steers her back to the contract award. She explains that it was a typical bidding process and, of course, she was very pleased to have been awarded the work. Really there was nothing very remarkable about it. She was particularly pleased with the pitch which her team had put together and which she had delivered in Mbombela. It was that which had clinched it she was sure. She guesses, Thabo knows, that Hadida was not the lowest bid.

Thabo enquires about the interactions she had with Mrs Pretty Mthembu and Lucas Nozulu. Pumza describes the hands-on role played by Lucas and casually drops in her entertainment of Pretty. Again, nothing remarkable when developing relationships with Government officials. Would it be considered normal for her to pick up the officials' expenses during a business trip to Cape Town, Thabo wonders. Pumza thinks so, provided there is some reciprocal gesture in the future. Thabo asks her if she has a credit card with the last four digits shown on Pretty's Cape Town hotel bill. Without hesitation, she admits that she does and makes no attempt to deny that she had made the payment. Thabo asks about any other payments made during the bidding process that he should know about. Pumza cannot think of any.

Thabo refers back to Pumza's mention of Oil & Gas and ask her if Hadida has links with a Services company owned by XaiXai Investments. Pumza does not think so but maybe one of her Business Development Managers would know. She can get back to him. Then he asks if her husband is involved in the business in any way. The question seems to unsettle Pumza briefly but she quickly recovers her poise and is emphatic in her denial. Junior is not involved in her business. He is far too busy with his ministerial portfolio. Thabo senses that Pumza is not so fond of her husband.

Thabo is disappointed with himself. He is using up the time he can reasonably expect Pumza to give him without uncovering any evidence of wrong doing on her part. The entertainment of Pretty is above board, although he doubts that it could ever be fully reciprocated; certainly not with same degree of lavish extravagance. Pretty's fraudulent expense claims do not implicate Pumza. Probably Da Costa and XaiXai have bypassed Pumza and developed a relationship with her husband without her help. He cannot seem to find the angle that would expose the role of Junior in taking illegal payments. A foreign bank account may be difficult to pin down. Probably he will need to talk to Junior face to face. Maybe Doctor can help.

Chapter 34
The Bluff

Doctor is just off the phone to Thabo who has briefed him on the not altogether successful meeting with Junior's wife. They really have no evidence that Junior is the minister taking illegal payments from XaiXai but they each have the same gut feel that somehow Junior is involved. Doctor sits on the stoep of his Aunt's home with a mug of coffee and tries to string together a hypothesis that works. He tries some ideas that precede April, to whom, for some reason, he has assigned the corrupting influence. Probably it was because he liked the idea of a privileged white woman worming her way into the unsuspecting brain of a middle ranking official.

He recalls that Lucas has a long history of local activism with the ANC and he also has a nagging doubt about the lifestyle he and his wife have been able to enjoy given the extent of his corruption uncovered so far. Trying a new hypothesis, maybe Lucas and Junior are linked more directly. Maybe they met in some ANC meeting, perhaps years ago, and Lucas has been benefiting somehow from this connection with the more senior cadre. Lucas has seemed so ill-equipped for lying and violence since their first meeting when he and April had rescued him from the boot of his Polo. The rational action would have been to have left him to endure a horrible, lingering death. Maybe though, he has underestimated his ability to be economical with the truth.

Lucas picks up on the second attempt. He is home alone still and miserable as a result. He is not keen to talk to Doctor again, hence the first missed call, but his need to be involved in something overcomes his reluctance on the second call.

Doctor goes straight to the point and bluffs the extent of his knowledge by accusing Lucas outright of being Junior's accomplice and taking a cut of the monthly payments from XaiXai. The silence from Lucas ends with a long exhalation of breath. It is as if days of pent up tension has been released by Doctor's challenge. He does not need to say anything. Doctor knows what the wordless reply means. Then the long silence is broken by a stream of consciousness.

*

In July 1991 Lucas travelled to Durban for the first National Conference since the ANC had been unbanned the previous year. He had been picked as one of the delegates for the Transvaal. This was a surprise to him because he had only been a member for about a year and he was not really so ambitious. Most of his work was in the invisible rural areas of the Lowveld, hundreds of kilometres from the big cities. Without really trying, he had come to the notice of the provincial leadership. He had been successful in recruiting many new members from the townships surrounding Nelspruit and he was outspoken about community issues in meetings the party organised with the municipalities in his Eastern Transvaal. People started to come to him with their problems. These, of course, were the very people who would unquestioningly vote for the ANC when the time came.

The trip to Durban was exciting for the young Lucas. First the journey south then east, in a minibus with seven of his colleagues, taking most of a day through scenery which changed from the rolling lawns of the Lowveld to the dramatic peaks of the Drakensberg and then descending rapidly to the Ocean. He saw

146

snow for the first time on the distant mountains of Lesotho. Lucas was stunned by the deep blue vista that opened up as they approached the City. The waves were flecked with white horses driven by the stiff wind. The sea air was warm even on this mid-winter day.

Lucas and his colleagues stayed in a guest house outside the centre of the city. They were bussed into the Conference Hall the next morning after a filling breakfast. It was a raucous gathering with groups dancing in the aisles dressed in ANC black, gold and green. Lucas had never fully appreciated the scale of the organisation that had successfully beaten the National Party into submission. He still held doubts that the white Government would relinquish power without a fight but he felt the energy of a people that knew that right was on their side. The big beasts of the Party were there and spoke passionately; Nelson Mandela, Walter Sisulu and Joe Slovo. Lucas was particularly impressed by Chris Hani, the leader of the armed wing of the ANC, Umkhonto we Sizwe, which was observing a cease fire.

During a fringe meeting which Lucas attended on the second evening, he met one of the mingling leaders who seemed to take an interest in him. Lucas was flattered to be asked about his work on behalf of the party. He nervously explained his recruitment work and the success he had taking issues to the local municipalities and getting small but important things done; long awaited water and electricity connections. He described the difficulties he encountered in generating belief in the membership who could not imagine a future in which they had a real say in the running of their country. Nevertheless, when disbelief was suspended, there was a powerful and seductive vision of a South

Africa where black citizens would be properly educated and have opportunities, until now, only dreamed of.

Lucas's deep voice carried more authority than he realised and combined with his slightly overweight build, he left a strong impression on the people he met.

The leader's interest seemed to wane after a few minutes and he moved on to another group of members but not before he took a note of Lucas's name.

It was ten years before Lucas met Junior Khumalo again. By 2001, Lucas was a Procurement Specialist in the Mpumalanga Provincial Government and Junior had recently been appointed to a junior ministerial role in Home Affairs. They met when Junior came to the Lowveld with other members of the Parliamentary Committee on Social Development. Lucas was invited to a reception for the visiting Parliamentarians. Junior came over and greeted Lucas as if they were old friends. Junior took his elbow and steered him to a quiet corner of the room. He asked him how he was finding life in the Administration. Lucas outlined his work and gave the impression of a man interested and motivated by what he was doing. The discussion moved on to his young family and how life was for them. Lucas was enjoying a modest but comfortable lifestyle that his parents could not have imagined. He had a wife, two children and a small home in Nelspruit, as it was still called. He was content. He really wanted for nothing except maybe a better car one day to advertise to his friends that he had made it. He camouflaged this thought with an uncharacteristically boyish giggle. Meanwhile, his faithful Toyota Corolla was sharp. Junior listened carefully and picked up on the automotive aspiration.

Maybe he could help with that. He had a friend in the business. The two men exchanged business cards.

A week later, Lucas got a call in his office from the car dealer that Junior had mentioned. He had heard that he might be in the market for a car. The dealer had just bought a repossessed BMW M3 at auction and Lucas could have it for a knock down price. Lucas could not afford even the low price and told the dealer so immediately. But his mind was already being messed with. The normally sensible Lucas now started to daydream of his life with the impressive vehicle parked outside his home. He would be the envy of his neighbours. He would need some new sunglasses and a sports shirt to complete the picture of affluence.

The dealer called back a couple of days later and asked if he had thought any more about the car. Lucas, still in his right mind, said that he really could not afford it; maybe in a couple of years. The dealer expressed disappointment but broached a new subject. Perhaps Lucas could help him. The Province was replacing its small fleet of Mpumalanga Government plated cars used by officials in their day to day work. The dealer wanted to be considered as a bidder but his business did not meet all the qualifying criteria. Could Lucas help to get his company included on the bid list? If so, the dealer would offer him the car for half the price already mentioned. Lucas's imagination was already in the driving seat heading for church with his family on a Sunday morning. His friends would be speechless when they saw him easing himself out of the air conditioned, leather upholstered luxury of his new wheels. The gospel music emanating loudly from the cool inside would attest to his continued, even reinforced, faith.

Two weeks later the car was delivered. The car came with the personalised registration plate that he would keep on successive vehicles including the more restrained but fully loaded Audi that he had been driving for the last year.

Next, the dealer needed his help to win the bid and when Lucas expressed his reluctance to assist, he calmly pointed out the difficulty Lucas would have explaining the M3 if its provenance were to be investigated. The dealer won the business and thirty white Toyotas were delivered shortly afterwards. Had anybody asked, they would have discovered that the small fleet was acquired, used, from a car rental company although the unit supply cost to the Province was not very different from a new car that a franchised dealer would have offered a private customer. Nobody asked.

After that, Lucas enjoyed several months of peace and he began to believe that his flirtation with corruption was just that. That was until he received an unexpected invitation for him and Pardon to spend the weekend with Junior and his wife at their new Sandton home. Lucas toyed with turning the invitation down but he made the mistake of mentioning it to Pardon. She was taken in by the idea of a luxurious break and finally he relented and emailed his acceptance.

The weekend in Sandton was lavish. The opulence of the Khumalo residence was outside the experience of Lucas and Pardon. The house party included three other couples. One of the couples were Portuguese and had flown up for the weekend from Maputo. They seemed to be keen to establish a friendship with the Nozulus. Pardon was quickly telling her life story to Anna Da Costa. Lucas found Luis Da Costa hard work; he tended to get overawed by successful people who had that easy way when socialising. He had to convince himself repeatedly that he belonged in this circle. Pardon, on the other hand, was warming to the task. She was much more gregarious than her husband and rapidly integrated with the group.

On the Sunday, Junior asked Lucas to join him in his office with Da Costa. Junior took the lead in the impromptu meeting using the authority that came from being host as well as his position in Government. He offered the two men a whisky. Da Costa seemed comfortable in the leather-bound office, warming the liquid in the crystal glass in his palm. Lucas felt far from comfortable. He had never got the taste for spirits and preferred a cold beer. Anyway, it was not even lunchtime.

Junior opened casually and suggested that he had enjoyed the weekend which he hoped they could repeat. He wanted to make a proposal that they each could think about over the next week or so.

The country was growing fast and there were so many opportunities to take just a small share of the spoils of that growth. This was a once in a lifetime opportunity and it would be a sin if they did not take advantage and make some money to make up for the wasted years of their youth. Lucas shifted uneasily in the oversized chair. He did not think like this. He remembered his father breaking his back in someone else's garden for subsistence wages, being insulted by a policeman, unable to afford a doctor for his sick mother. For him, life was so incomparably better.

The outline of the proposal involved Da Costa as the front man for a range of businesses in Southern Africa that could provide services to Provincial and National Government. Lucas's role was to facilitate contract awards in his own Province as well as using his network to make recommendations to colleagues in other Provinces. He would be paid a retainer and a percentage of the value of contracts in which he played a successful role. It would also be helpful if Lucas's wife could join the boards of several of the businesses that were to be registered in South Africa. She too would receive a salary for her non-executive services.

Lucas promised to give the proposal some serious thought and to discuss it with Pardon.

On the drive home, Lucas had broached the subject with Pardon, expecting her to be shocked and disapproving. In fact, she was quite receptive. She had got a taste for the kind of life that her new-found friends enjoyed and she felt that it was time that Lucas's hard work was rewarded.

*

Doctor hears a sigh of relief at the other end of the line. Doctor has been standing for the whole of Lucas's breathless account, tensing as it reached its conclusion and now he collapses back into the old chair on the stoep. His coffee is cold. He feels a sense of anti-climax. It seems like he has unravelled the story and that there is not much more to find out. He realises that Junior's corruption probably extends way beyond the relationship with Lucas and Da Costa but now the Hawks will need to take over and his involvement is unlikely to be welcome.

Chapter 35
The Bargain

Thabo is making another visit to the Nozulu home. This time he has his deputy with him. They are expected. Pardon is back, clearly still angry and cold. She opens the door and leads them through to the study where Lucas has his attorney with him. Thabo had the full story from Doctor the previous evening. He wastes no time telling Lucas that the evidence of his link to the Government minister, Junior Khumalo is mounting up. His deputy adds to the pressure by suggesting that the extent of Lucas's corruption will translate into a long jail sentence and the confiscation of his remaining assets.

Lucas, on the instruction of his lawyer, makes no comment. He looks crushed. His eyes are red from lack of sleep. His clothes are crumpled; he has not ironed his own clothes for many years and clearly, he has not made the effort now. Pardon is certainly not in the mood for traditional housewife duties and is increasingly resentful that their domestic worker is no longer around.

Thabo, his eyes ranging between those of Lucas and his attorney, makes his proposal. A long jail sentence might be avoided and Pardon could be given immunity if Lucas turned state witness against Junior Khumalo. Lucas might be sentenced to a 5 year stretch but could reckon on release after three years. The lawyer asks about the Nozulu assets. The house is in Pardon's name. Thabo is non-committal; just repeating that Pardon will be offered immunity.

The lawyer requests some time for consideration and promises to call Thabo in the next few hours. Lucas looks shell shocked. It is one of several moments of truth in the last month. His fall is nearly complete. Only the humiliation of his trial and his appearance in the role of star witness is now needed to finish the job. He kicks himself again for the greedy side show he set up with April which added very little to the considerable wealth he has accumulated with the more sophisticated deals involving Khumalo and Da Costa. It was the sideshow that Doctor first uncovered. April's murder ensured that the investigation would not be contained.

The meeting has lasted less than ten minutes and the two Hawks are back in their car. They know that Lucas has no choice. He will take the plea bargain deal. It is only a few more minutes before the lawyer calls to agree in principle and to request a meeting with Thabo's lawyers to fill out the details.

Chapter 36
Dénouement

Junior and Pumza Khumalo are together at home for the first time in weeks. Over breakfast, Junior appears agitated. Pumza persuades him to open up. Reluctantly, he shares his concern that his relationship with Da Costa is unravelling. Pumza in turn relates her meeting with Thabo. She feels that she handled it well and suggests that the Hawks have nothing beyond the corrupt Procurement people in Mpumalanga. Junior retells the Sunday Times' version of the XaiXai story. Pumza now remembers the headline shouting out of the supermarket shelves a couple of Sundays ago but she makes it a rule not to read the newspapers when she is on holiday. The connection to their Mozambican partners had passed her by until now. Junior does not mention his historic link with the investigative journalist. Pumza is completely unaware of her husband's act of betrayal and role as a double agent during the Struggle.

Junior is anxious that he has been unable to reach Da Costa to understand from him just how badly their relationship has been exposed. His attempts to talk to Lucas have also been unsuccessful. Pumza's advice is to assume that they are going to be exposed and that the priority now should be to cover their tracks as best as possible. Junior has already been thinking along these lines. He has deleted an e-mail account that he reserved for his questionable business dealings. The foreign bank accounts that he holds will certainly be discovered but he has shredded statements nevertheless. He has deleted the contacts he would prefer the Hawks not to know about and changed the SIM card in his phone. The frenetic activity lasts for about an hour and then subsides into despondency. He has formed a clear idea that there is no future beyond today.

At the same time, Thabo has one of his analysts downloading Junior's phone records and another pulling his last five years' tax returns. Junior's efforts to cover his tracks will be useless. It will take a while to identify his foreign bank accounts but the couple's lifestyle will have required funds beyond that declared so the evidence will not take a major forensic effort to collect.

In her study, Pumza books a flight to Dubai leaving that evening. She pays for the flight with the credit card linked to an account in the Emirate which she holds jointly with Junior. She packs a cabin bag and tells her assistant at Hadida to hold the fort for her. She does not say where she is going or how long she will be away.

Pumza drives herself to Rosebank telling Junior she is going shopping. She leaves her car in the station car park and takes the Gautrain to the airport. She checks in about four hours before her flight is due to take off. The officer at the emigration checkpoint, looks at her suspiciously as she swipes her passport. Instead of passing the passport back to her, she picks up the phone. A few seconds later, two officers arrive and ask Pumza to accompany them.

Junior locks his office door and sits down at his desk to write a letter to Doctor. Mid-way through this confession he pauses and takes himself back four decades to the Sunday afternoon at the Zoo Lake. He tries to recreate the idealistic Junior of that time but realises that he did not exist. He was only ever an opportunist. His relative innocence on the day that he intervened on behalf of the handsome, harassed young couple was bound to be sullied by the pervasive corruption that coexisted with Apartheid. He was and is still just the kind of man that such corruption feeds on. The Doctor that he had betrayed was not well educated. Ironically, the low expectations that held him back would also have helped to keep him honest had he lived longer.

Junior sighs, disappointed that his thoughts have not surfaced some good personal quality that he could cling to amongst the wreckage of his life. He returns to his letter.

The Khumalo housekeeper is taking her afternoon nap in her room ahead of serving Junior tea as is his routine at four every afternoon when he is not at the Union Buildings or sitting in Parliament when in session in Cape Town. She is restless because the atmosphere in the house is palpably malevolent. As she is rousing herself, she hears a loud report. A gunshot. She rushes to Junior's study. Unable to get in, she calls the guard at the gate who struggles but eventually breaks down the door. The housekeeper follows him in and is horrified by what she sees. Her employer is slumped over his desk in a pool of blood which is expanding, darkly glistening, as she watches. The letter addressed to a Doctor Lukhele at The Sunday Times is on the desk, beyond the expanding red tide and unbloodied.

*

Junior's last thoughts, as he sealed the envelope containing his confession, centred on his second betrayal. The one after Doctor. It was these thoughts that helped him pull the trigger. He was in Zambia a couple of months after his journey into exile. He was settling into the ANC compound in Lusaka and discovering the suburb and its shops and bars. He had almost forgotten the obligation he was now under and hoped that the security forces back home had forgotten too.

One late morning he was sitting in his new favourite bar nursing a beer when he was joined by a white man who he immediately recognised as the BOSS officer he had met in John Vorster Square. The man appeared to be wearing the same grubby, creased shirt that he had on the day of their first encounter. This time though he had found time for a shave. The BOSS man ordered a beer for himself and looked away into the middle distance while enquiring about Junior's wellbeing. Without waiting for an answer, he went on to say that he was aware of the imminent arrival of a senior Mozambican government adviser. He needed to get hold of the itinerary. He was sure Junior could help. The officer's beer arrived but he was already gone. He would meet Junior the next morning and pick up the intelligence he needed.

A week later, a Special Forces team would tape an explosive package together with its altitude activated detonator to the advisor's plane as it stood on the tarmac in Beira, engines running, ready to taxi.

The many subsequent betrayals were archived deep in his memory and no amount of procrastination with the gun would allow him to dredge them to the surface. Nor would there be any point.

Chapter 37
The Letter

Doctor is back in Johannesburg and sitting in the smart, glass wrapped, Parktown office of his Editor. He is dressed in a new crisp white shirt and black jeans with the kind of fit that accentuate his height. The sun blinds are down against the early summer glare. The cotton wool, Highveld clouds drift gently across the Northern Suburbs. An intern brings him a coffee. There is a look of admiration on his face which mirrors those he received from some of the staff in the news room as he walked in.

The Editor comes into the office accompanied by a smartly dressed older man who introduces himself as General Counsel. The corporate lawyer hands him a letter. Doctor is expecting a job offer but he realises immediately that it is something else. The Editor explains it is a letter from Junior Khumalo written just before his suicide. The police have taken a copy. Doctor is not sure what to do next. Should he read it while they watch? He opens the envelope and pulls out three closely filled sheets of stiff letter-writing paper. They exude a faint reminder of stale cigar smoke. Why had Junior written personally to him? It was easy to imagine that killing himself was the only way out but why write to a journalist he had never met?

Doctor starts to scan the letter and then returns to its beginning and reads carefully. The letter is Junior's story starting with his interrogation in John Vorster Square. The death of Doctor's father makes sense for the first time. He begins to weep. He passes the letter to the Editor who starts again reading aloud. The trio in the office descend into a state of deep shock. It is as if a bomb has just exploded; although to describe this confession as a bombshell scarcely does it justice. The letter ends with a humble apology to Doctor and, more ostentatiously, to the people of South Africa.

Doctor leaves the office, recovers his still faithful Polo and heads south towards his Mother's home in Soweto. Lefa answers the door and flings her arms around her son's neck. She has spoken to him on the phone since his return from Mozambique but this is their first meeting since the weekend in KaBokweni which seems an age ago. She had fretted about his safety and lost a lot of sleep but now she is happy to find her handsome son looking in good shape and dressed like the successful, sober man that he now is.

Doctor, sitting with Lefa and nursing a mug of tea, hands her the letter. Lefa searches for her reading glasses and then not knowing what to expect, starts to read the explosive story which had changed her life more than forty years earlier. Her first Doctor had inexplicably failed to return from his bit part in the Soweto protests. Now, at last, she understands why. She lets out a piercing scream and sobs uncontrollably for the second time in Doctor's recollection. He, his Father's legacy, puts his big arms around her shoulders to comfort her.

Chapter 38
Loose Ends

The veteran activist, whose hotel bill triggered Doctor's investigation, is babysitting his grandchildren at home while avidly consuming The Sunday Times. Abu is angry but unsurprised to read about Junior Khumalo's traitorous activities. Maybe his demise will mark the beginning of a much-needed clean-up. More likely it will send a small but damaging group of the newly rich into a frenzy of cover up. Still, he reflects, it is a step in the right direction. He clears his throat and picks up the phone to call SAFM. He has plenty to say.

Joy Mpofu is making the finishing touches to the family Sunday lunch. Her whistleblowing role is still known only to Abu, Doctor and the Hawks. She is quite happy to keep it that way.

Pumza Khumalo is being driven from the police cell she has occupied for the last three days to Johannesburg Prison in the south of the city. She had been remanded in custody two days earlier; considered a flight risk. Then, her lawyer had broken the terrible news about Junior. She has been unable to cry. On arrival at the prison, she is handed an orange jump suit that feels horribly coarse. She removes her jewellery and a Chopard wrist watch which the female warder takes from her and places in a plastic bag before sealing and labelling it. Once in the jump suit, her body itches terribly. She is led to a cell. While she is on remand, probably for months, she will be held in solitary confinement. The cell is spartan but clean. A narrow bed and an army blanket on one side, a toilet and sink in the far corner below a barred window. There is a scrubbed wooden desk and chair. She finds a

Bible in the drawer. Now she cries; not for Junior, but for the lost luxury that she will not be enjoying for years to come, perhaps.

Funi is relaxing in her yard after Church. Precious is grumbling about his new status as one of the many unemployed in the area. Tomorrow he will join his brother and stand on a street corner in White River in the hope of picking up some casual labouring. Funi is not so worried. Doctor has given her some money; notionally as payment for his lodgings but in fact much more than she would have expected. The family will be alright for at least a month.

Doctor and Hlengiwe, also fresh out of Church, are driving out to their favourite restaurant to celebrate Doctor's success. The Sunday Times on the back seat has a front-page headline story and an inside double page spread, written entirely by Doctor; a detailed exposé of Minister Junior Khumalo. Doctor's Polo is humming smoothly as if to emphasise that, although an upgrade is now eminently affordable, it is entirely unnecessary.

Doctor is planning to discuss the decision he needs to make; joining the staff of the Sunday Times would be a dream come true but take him away from the Lowveld where his roots have started to take hold. The couple sit outside under a sun awning and take time over their food. Their talk starts lightly, skirting the dramas of the last month. It then moves to the future. Their future. They both agree their relationship is still in its infancy and past experience tells them that they should not rush into next steps. Doctor makes sure Hlengiwe knows how much he has fallen for her and she responds with a wide smile and, as is now familiar, her signature hand to the back of his head. She does not really need his reassurance.

Doctor raises the issue of his job offer. Hlengiwe is sure he should take it. They can get together regularly and let their relationship grow slowly. The decision, which might have caused Doctor to agonize in the past, or even resort to the bottle, is taken in a few seconds.

Thabo Mkhize is reading through the file that his team have compiled on "The Mozambican Connection" as they have been calling the case. He will make a few minor edits and on Monday morning the file will go to the National Prosecution Authority. He is angry at the suicide of Junior which will preclude meaningful investigation of others in high places. The anger will subside quickly. Thabo is already anticipating his next case.

Luis Da Costa is settling into his business class seat for the overnight TAP flight to Lisbon. He tucks the false passport, with which he passed through emigration, into the laptop carrier that he slings up into the overhead bin. The steward brings him a glass of champagne. He sips it appreciatively and thinks about the last month. A life of increasingly easy luxury had suddenly turned ugly and violent. His partner, Francisco, had died at XaiXai. His wife is already in Portugal. Most of his fortune is in a private Madeira bank and he has a large plot of land there on which he plans to build an imposing villa. Doctor Lukhele will not easily follow him there. The South African Police and the Hawks will circulate his details through Interpol but if he is careful he can evade arrest. It is probably time to retire and enjoy the fruits of his criminal labour. Junior's suicide is regrettable but at the same time rather satisfactory.

The northbound plane accelerates down the runway, takes off and heads out over the azure Indian Ocean before turning back inland, settling onto its course, and flying over XaiXai. Looking west, Da Costa sees blood-soaked thunder clouds over the distant escarpment. He reclines, puts on his headphones and selects a recently released movie; a romantic comedy.

Doctor and Hlengiwe are lingering over their coffee, enjoying each other's company. The tensions of the last week have evaporated and the not so difficult decision has been made. It is late afternoon and the same storm clouds, that Da Costa had seen in the distance from his plane, are building and climbing rapidly over the adjacent hills. A sudden, dry wind sends them indoors and a few minutes later it starts to rain. Large, infrequent drops turn quickly into a deluge. The summer rains have arrived. The Lowveld will soon be a lush green again.

Glossary

ANC	The African National Council - the liberation movement founded in 1912.
CIPRO	Companies and Intellectual Property Registration Office; now renamed CIPC - Companies and Intellectual Property Commission.
Egoli	Johannesburg (*Zulu*) - Place of Gold (more properly eGoli).
eish	Expression of exasperation used by everyone in South Africa.
goggas	Insects (*Afrikaans*)
gogo	Grandmother (from *Zulu* ugogo)
kopje	Small hill common in the Highveld (*Afrikaans* "little head").
LM Prawns	Lourenço Marques Prawns - Portuguese style prawns cooked in Peri-Peri sauce.
location	Township for non-whites; The Apartheid regime created locations and forcibly removed non-white people from cities and towns as legislated for in The Group Areas Act 1950.
magwinya	A deep-fried doughnut, also called fat cake.
mealy pap	Staple food and popular braai (barbeque) food made from maize meal and water.
necklacing	Form of execution practiced against alleged Apartheid regime collaborators; involved filling a tyre with petrol, placing over the victim's head and setting it alight.
padkos	road food (Afrikaans); no South African travels without it.

PUTCO	Pretoria Urban Transport Company
robot	traffic Light
SAP	South African Police - Apartheid era
SAPS	South African Police Service - Democratic era
sarmie	sarnie – sandwich
sawubona	hello (*Zulu*), literally meaning "I see you, you are important to me and I value you".
sharp	Fine, OK
sjambok	Heavy leather whip carried by SA Police. It is traditionally made from hippopotamus or rhinoceros hide, now commonly plastic
spaza shop	Informal shop in townships; often run by immigrants and selling day to day necessities and airtime.
tekkies	Trainers/sports shoes
yebo	An exclamation used to show agreement or approval; yes

Short Stories by Peter Lewis in Kindle Reader Format:

Short Stories from the Lowveld of South Africa
1. Privilege
2. Funi
3. Doctor

Monsoon Monday – A Short Story from Myanmar

Printed in Great Britain
by Amazon

82426968R00098